Jeremy Belknap

The Foresters

An American Tale

Jeremy Belknap

The Foresters
An American Tale

ISBN/EAN: 9783337375867

Printed in Europe, USA, Canada, Australia, Japan

Cover: Foto ©Andreas Hilbeck / pixelio.de

More available books at **www.hansebooks.com**

THE
FORESTERS,

AN

AMERICAN TALE:

BEING A

SEQUEL TO THE HISTORY

OF

JOHN BULL the CLOTHIER.

In a SERIES of LETTERS to a FRIEND.

Published according to Act of Congress.

THE SECOND EDITION,
REVISED AND CONSIDERABLY ENLARGED.

PRINTED at *BOSTON*,
BY I. THOMAS AND E. T. ANDREWS,
[PROPRIETORS of the WORK.]

Sold by them, *J. White, D. West,* and *E. Larkin,* in Boston; by *Thomas, Son & Thomas,* in Worcester; by *Thomas, Andrews & Butler,* in Baltimore; and by *Thomas, Andrews & Penniman,* in Albany.——*Nov.* 1796.

CONTENTS.

LETTER

C O N T E N T S. v

LETTER

LETTER.

Bull's

CLAVIS ALLEGORICA.

⚫●◆●◆●⚫

JOHN BULL, *The Kingdom of England.*
—His MOTHER, *The Church of England.*
—His WIFE, *The Parliament.*
—His SISTER PEG, *The Church of Scotland.*
—His BROTHER PATRICK, *Ireland.*
LEWIS, *The Kingdom of France.*
—His MISTRESS, *The Old Constitution.*
—His NEW WIFE, *The National Representation.*
LORD STRUT, *The Kingdom of Spain.*
NICHOLAS FROG, *The Dutch Republic.*
GUSTAVUS, *The Kingdom of Sweden.*
MADAM KATE, *The Empire of Russia.*
LEOPOLD, *The Empire of Germany.*
FREDERICK, *The Prussian Monarchy.*
FERDINAND, *The Dutchy of Brunswick.*
CANG-HI, *The Empire of China.*
THE FRANKS, *The French Republic.*
THE FORESTERS, *The United States of America.*
ALEXANDER SCOTUS, *Nova Scotia.*
ONONTIO, *Canada.*
ROBERT LUMBER, *New Hampshire.*
JOHN CODLINE, *Massachusetts.*
PEREGRINE PICKLE, *The Old Colony of Plymouth.*
THEOPHILUS WHEAT-EAR, *The Old Col. of New Haven.*
HUMPHRY PLOUGHSHARE, *Connecticut.*
ROGER CARRIER, *Rhode Island and Providence.*
PETER BULL-FROG, *New York.*
JULIUS CESAR, *New Jersey.*
CART-RUT and BARE-CLAY, *Carteret and Barclay.*

WILLIAM

B

WILLIAM BROADBRIM,	*Pennſylvania.*
———— CASIMIR,	*Delaware.*
CECILIUS MARYGOLD,	*Maryland.*
WALTER PIPEWEED,	*Virginia.*
—His GRANDSON,	*GEORGE WASHINGTON.*
PETER PITCH,	*North Carolina.*
CHARLES INDIGO,	*South Carolina.*
GEORGE TRUSTY,	*Georgia.*
AUGUSTINE,	*Florida.*
ETHAN GREENWOOD,	*Vermont.*
HUNTER LONGKNIFE,	*Kentucky.*
HIGHWAYMEN,	*Pirates and Privateers.*
HOUNDS AND HUNTSMEN,	*Ships of War and Troops.*
BEARS AND WOLVES,	*Indians.*
BLACK CATTLE,	*Negro Slaves.*
RATS,	*Speculators.*
MOTHER CAREY'S CHICKENS,	*Jacobins.*
ORDURE,	*Convicts.*

THE

FORESTERS.

Letter I.

*Original State of the Foreſt.—The Adven-
tures of* WALTER PIPEWEED *and* CE-
CILIUS PETERSON.

DEAR SIR,

To perform the promiſe which I
made to you before I began my journey, I
will give you ſuch an account of this,
once foreſt, but now cultivated and pleaſ-
ant country, as I can collect from my con-
verſation with its inhabitants, and from
the peruſal of their old family papers,

B 2   which

which they have kindly permitted me to look into for my entertainment. By thefe means I have acquainted myfelf with the ftory of their firft planting, confequent improvements, and prefent ftate; the re-cital of which will occupy the hours which I fhall be able to fpare from bufinefs, com-pany and fleep, during my refidence among them.

In reading the character of *John Bull*, which was committed to paper fome years ago by one who knew him well, you muft have obferved, that though "he was in the main an honeft, plain dealing fellow, yet he was choleric and inconftant, and very apt to *quarrel with his beft friends.*" This obfervation you will find fully verified in the courfe of the narrative; and as the opinions and manners of fuperiors have a very great influence in forming the char-acter of inferiors, you need not be fur-prifed if you find a family likenefs pre-vailing among the perfons whofe hiftory I

am

am about to recite, most of whom were formerly residents in Mr. Bull's house, or apprentices in his shop.

THERE was among the appendages to John's estate, a pretty large tract of land, which had been neglected by his ancestors, and which he never cared much about, excepting that now and then some of his family went thither a hunting, and brought home venison and furs.   Indeed this was, as far as I can find, the best pretence that John had to call the land his; for he had no legal title to it.   It was then a very woody country, in some parts rocky and hilly, in other parts level; well watered with brooks and ponds, and the whole of it bordered on a large lake, in which were plenty of fish, some of which were often served up at John's table, on fast days.

THE stories told by one and another of these adventurers, had made a deep impression on the mind of *Walter Pipeweed*, one
of

of John's domeſtics, a fellow of a roving
and projecting diſpoſition, and who had
learned the art of ſurveying. · Walter having frequently liſtened to their chat, began
to think within himſelf, "If theſe fellows
make ſo many pence by their excurſions to
this wild ſpot, what might not I gain by ſitting down upon it? There is plenty of
game and fiſh at hand, for a preſent ſupply;
plenty of nuts and acorns to fatten· pigs,
and with ſome ſmall labour I may be able
to raiſe corn and feed poultry, which will
fetch me a good price at market.—I can
carry biſket enough in my pockets to keep
me alive till my firſt crop comes in, and my
dog can live upon the offals of the game
that I ſhall kill.—Beſides, who knows what
treaſures the land itſelf may contain—perhaps ſome *rich mines !*—then I am made
for this world—I ſhall be as rich as *Lord
Strut !*

· FULL of this dream, Walter applied to
his maſter one day for a leaſe of part of

                                                the

the foreft, as it was called. Bull at firft laughed at the propofal, and put him off; but Walter followed it up fo clofe, and told what advantages might be gained by fettling there, and promifed, if he fhould fucceed, to turn all his trade into his mafter's hand, and give him the refufal of whatever he might bring to market, and withal fhewed him fome drafts, which he had made with chalk, from the reports of the huntfmen, that Bull began to think of the matter in good earneft, and confulted his lawyer upon the fubject, who, after due confideration of the premifes, and ftroking his band, advifed him as follows. "Why yes, Mr. Bull, I don't fee why you ought not to look about you as well as your neighbours. You know that old *Lord Peter* lays claim to the whole country, and has affumed to parcel it out among his devotees. He has given all the weftern part of it, where this foreft lies, to *Lord Strut*, and he has a large manor adjoining to your foreft, which, they fay, yields him a fine rent, and

who

who knows but this may bring you in as much, or more?——Then there is *Lewis*, the cudgel player, and *Nicholas Frog*, the draper, who have, perhaps, (I say *perhaps*, Mr. Bull, because there may be a little doubt on both sides, and in that case, you know Sir, it would not become gentlemen of our cloth to speak positively) as good a claim as your Honor to this land; but then it is a maxim, you know, that possession is eleven points of the law, and if you once get your foot upon it, they cannot oust you without a process, and your Honor knows that your purse is as long as theirs, and you are as able to stand a suit with them as they are with you. I therefore advise you to humour your man Walter, and give him a lease, and a pretty large one—you may find more advantages in it than you are aware of—but lease it, lease it, at any rate." Upon this he was ordered to make out a lease; and Walter being thus invested with as good authority as could be obtained, filled his pockets with bread and cheese, took

his

his gun, powder-flask, and shot of various kinds, with a parcel of fishing-lines and hooks, his surveying instruments, and a bag of corn on his shoulders, and off he trotted to his new paradise.

It was some time before he could fix upon a spot to his liking, and he at first met with some opposition from the bears and wolves, and was greatly exposed to the weather, before he could build him a hut; once or twice the savage animals had almost devoured him, but being made of good stuff, he stood his ground, cleared a little spot, put his seed into the earth, and lived as well as such adventurers can expect, poorly e-nough at first, but supported, as all new planters are, by the hope of better times. After a while he began to thrive, and his master Bull recommended a *wife*,* whom he married, and by whom he had a number of children. Having found a new sort of grain in the forest, and a certain plant of a narcotic quality, he cultivated both, and

having

* The charter of Virginia.

having procured a number of *black cattle,* he went on pretty gaily in the planting way, and brought his narcotic weed into great repute, by sending a present of a quantity of it to his old master, who grew excessively fond of it, and kept calling for more, till he got the whole trade of it into his own hands, and sold it out of his own warehouse to Lewis, Frog, and all the other tradesmen around him. In return, he supplied Walter with cloths and stuffs for his family, and utensils for his husbandry; and as a reward for being the first, who had courage to make a settlement in his forest, he dignified his plantation with the name of the *ancient dominion.* Beside this mark of respect, and in token of his high esteem of him as a customer, as well as for certain other reasons, he made it a practice, every year, to present him with a waggon load of *Ordure,* the sweepings of his back yard, the scrapings of his dog kennel, and contents of his own water closet. This was a mark of politeness which John valued himself

much

much upon. " It may feem odd (faid he one day to a friend) that I make fuch a kind of compliment as this to my good cuftomer; but if you confider it aright, you will find it a piece of refined policy; for by this means I get rid of a deal of trafh and rubbifh that is neceffarily made in fuch a family as mine; I get a curfed ftink removed from under my nofe, and my good friend has the advantage of it upon his farm, to manure his grounds, and make them produce more plentifully that precious weed in which we all fo much delight." Walter was often feen, on the arrival of Bull's waggon, to clap his handkerchief to his nofe; but as he knew his old mafter was an odd fort of a fellow, and it was his intereft to keep in with him, he generally turned off the compliment with a laugh, faying, good-naturedly enough, " Let him laugh that wins," without explaining his meaning, though it might admit of a *double entendre*; then calling fome of his fervants, he ordered them to fhovel out the dung,

and

and make his black cattle mix theirs with it. When spread over the land, the air took out most of the scent, and the salts were of some advantage to the soil.

AFTER Walter Pipeweed had got his affairs into tolerable order, he was visited in his retirement by *Cecilius Peterson*,* another of Bull's apprentices, who had taken a fancy to the same kind of life, from a disgust to some things that had happened in the family. He had not been long with Walter before he found it would not do for him to remain there. Peterson was supposed to be a natural son of old *Lord Peter*, after whom he was nick-named. He had the same affected airs, and a tincture of the high-flying notions of his reputed father. These made him rather disgustful to Walter, who had learned his manners of Mr. Bull's mother, when she was in her sober senses,

* Lord Baltimore, who first settled Maryland, was a Papist; his successors abjured Popery, and conformed to the Church of England.

senses, and between her and Lord Peter there had been a long variance. When Peterson perceived that his company was not desired, he had so much good sense as to leave Walter's plantation, and, paddling across a creek, seated himself on a point of land that ran out into the lake. Of this he obtained a lease of his old master, and went to work in the same manner as Walter had done, who, liking his company best at a distance, was willing to supply him with bread and meat till he could scramble for himself. Here he took to husbandry, raising corn and the narcotic weed, and buying up *black cattle*, and after a while turned his produce into his old master's ware-house, and received from him the annual compliment of a waggon load of dung, excepting that when there had not been so much as usual made, he and Walter were to share a load between them.

To ingratiate himself still farther with his old master, he accepted of a girl out of his family for a wife, (for John was always

fond

fond of his tenants marrying for fear of
their doing worfe) he took as little notice
as poffible of his reputed father, and drop-
ping, or difowning his nick-name of Peter-
fon, he affumed that of *Marygold*, which
old Madam Bull underftood as a compliment to one of her daughters.   He alfo
made his court to the old lady by kneeling
down and kiffing the golden fringe of her
embroidered petticoat, as was the fafhion
of that day. This ceremony, though a trifle
in itfelf, helped much to recommend him
to Mr. Bull, who was a very dutiful fon,
and took his mother's advice in moft parts
of his bufinefs.   In fhort, Cecilius was too
much of a politician to fuppofe that filial
affection ought to ftand in the way of a
man's intereft, and in this he judged as many other men would have done in the fame
circumftances.

Letter II.

Sickness and Delirium of Mr. BULL's *Mother.*
—Adventures of PEREGRINE PICKLE.—
JOHN CODLINE.—HUMPHRY PLOUGH-
SHARE.—ROGER CARRIER, *and* THE-
OPHILUS WHEAT-EAR.

DEAR SIR,

ABOUT the time in which these
first attempts were making, and the fame
of them had raised much jealousy among
some, and much expectation among others,
there happened a sad quarrel in *John Bull's*
family. His mother, poor woman, had
been seized with hysteric fits, which caused
her at times to be delirious and full of all
sorts of whims. She had taken it into her
head that every one of the family must hold
                                    knife

knife and fork and fpoon exactly alike; that
they muft all wafh their hands and face
precifely in the fame manner; that they
muft fit, ftand, walk, kneel, bow, fpit, blow
their nofes, and perform every other animal function by the exact rule of *uniformity*,
which fhe had drawn up with her own
hand, and from which they were not allowed to vary one hair's breadth. If any
one of the family complained of a lame an-
cle or ftiff knee, or had the crick in his neck,
or happened to cut his finger, or was any
other way fo difabled as not to perform his
duty to a tittle, fhe was fo far from making
the leaft allowance, that fhe would frown,
and fcold, and rave like a bedlamite; and
John was fuch an obedient fon to his mother, that he would lend her his hand to box
their ears, or his foot to kick their back-
fides, for not complying with her humour.
This way of proceeding raifed an uproar in
the family; for though moft of them com-
plied, either through affection for the old
lady, or through fear, or fome other motive,

yet

yet others looked four, and grumbled; some would openly find fault and attempt to remonstrate, but they were answered with a kick or a thump, or a cat-o'nine-tails, or shut up in a dark garret till they promised a compliance. Such was the logic of the family in those days!

AMONG the number of the disaffected, was *Peregrine Pickle*, a pretty clever sort of a fellow about his business, but a great lover of four crout, and of an humour that would not bear contradiction. However, as he knew it would be, fruitless to enter into a downright quarrel, and yet could not live there in peace; he had so much prudence as to quit the house, which he did by getting out of the window in the night. Not liking to be out of employment, he went to the house of *Nicholas Frog*, his master's old friend and rival, told him the story of his sufferings, and got leave to employ himself in one of his workshops till the storm should be over. After he had been here a while, he thought Nick's family were

C

as much too loofe in their manners as Bull's were too ftrict; and having heard a rumour of the Foreft, to which Nick had fome kind of claim, he packed up his little all, and hired one of Nick's fervants who had been there a hunting, to pilot him to that part of the Foreft to which Nick laid claim. But Frog had laid an anchor to windward of him; for as Pickle had faid nothing to him about a leafe, ' :: fuppofed that when Peregrine had got into the Foreft he would take a leafe of his old mafter Bull, which would ftrengthen his title, and weaken his own; he therefore bribed the pilot to fhew Peregrine to a barren part of the Foreft, inftead of that fertile place* to which he had already fent his furveyors, and of which he was contriving to get poffeffion. Accordingly the pilot having conducted Pickle to a fandy point which runs into the lake,† it being the dufk of the evening,‡ bade him good night, and walked off. Peregrine, who was fatigued with his

‑ march,

* Hudfon's River.　　† Cape Cod.
‡ The month of December.

march, laid down and went to fleep, but
waking in the morning, faw himfelf alone
in a very dreary fituation, where he could
get nothing to live upon but clams, and a
few acorns which the fquirrels had left. In
this piteous plight, the poor fellow folded
his arms, and walking along the fandy beach,
fell into fuch a foliloquy as this. "So
much for travelling! Abufed by Bull, cheat-
ed by Fron, what am I at laft come to?
Here I am alone, no creatures but bears,
and wolves, and fuch vermin around me!
Nothing in the fhape of an human being
that I know of, nearer than Pipeweed's plantation, and with him I cannot agree; he
is fo devoted to old Dame Bull that he and
I cannot live together any more than I
could with the old woman. But, why
fhould I defpair? That is unmanly; there
is at leaft a *poffibility* of my living here,
and if I am difappointed in my worldly
profpects, it is but right, for I profeffed
not to have any. My wifh was to have my
own way without difturbance or contradiction, and furely I can here enjoy my liber-

ty.

ty.   I have nobody here to curfe me, or
kick me, or cheat me.   If I have only clams
to eat, I can cook them my own way, and
fay as long a grace over them as I pleafe.
I can fit or ftand, or kneel, or ufe any other
pofture at my devotions, without any crofs
old woman to growl at me, or any hector-
ing bully to cuff me · for it.   So that if I
have loft in one way I have gained in another.   I had better therefore reconcile myfelf
to my fituation, and make the beft of a bad
market.   But company is good ! Apropos !
I will write to fome of my fellow-apprentices ; I know they were as difcontented as
myfelf in old Bull's family, though they
did not care to fpeak their minds as plainly
as I did.   I'll tell them how much happinefs I enjoy here in my folitude.   I'll point
out to them the charms of liberty, and coax
them to follow me into the wildernefs ;
and by and by, when we get all together,
we fhall make a brave hand of it."   Full of
this refolution, he fat down on a wind-fall-
en tree, and pulling out his inkhorn and paper, wrote a letter to *John Codline, Hum-*
phry

phry Ploughfhare, and *Roger Carrier*, three of his fellow-apprentices, informing them of the extreme happinefs he enjoyed in having liberty to eat his fcanty meals in his own way, and to lay his fwelled ancles and ftiff knee in whatever pofture was moft eafy to him; conjuring them by their former friendfhip, to come to join him in carrying on the good work fo happily begun, &c. &c. As foon as he had finifhed the letter, (which had deeply engaged his attention) a huntfman happened to come along in queft of game. This was a lucky circumftance indeed, for Peregrine had not once thought of a conveyance for his letter; it proved alfo favourable to him in another view, for the huntfman taking pity on his forlorn fituation, fpared him fome powder and fhot, and a few bifcuit which he happened to have in his pocket; fo taking charge of the letter, he delivered it as it was directed.

THIS letter arrived in good feafon, for old Madam had grown much worfe fince
Pickle

Pickle had left the family; her vapours had increafed, and her longings and aver- fions were much ftronger. ⸱ She had a ftrange lurch for embroidere'd petticoats and high waving plumes; her Chriftmas pies. muft have double the quantity of fpice that was ufual; the fervants muft make three bows where they formerly made but one, and they muft never come into her prefence. without having curled and powdered their hair in the pink of the mode, for fhe had an averfion to every thing plain, and a. ftrong relifh for every thing gaudy. Be- fides, fhe had an high-mettled chaplain* who was conftantly at her elbow, and faid. prayers night and morning in a brocaded. cope with a gilded mitre on his head; and he exacted fo many bows and fcrapes of ev- ery one in the family, that it would have puzzled a French dancing-mafter to have kept pace with him. Nor would he per- form the fervice at all, unlefs a verger ftood. by him all the while with a yard-wand in his hand; and if any fervant or apprentice miffed

* Archbifhop Laud.

miffed one bow or fcrape, or made it at the
wrong time, or dared to look off his book,
or faid Amen in the wrong place, rap went
the ftick over his head and ears or knuckles.
It was in vain to appeal from the chaplain
or the old Dame to their mafter, for he was
fo obedient a fon that he fuffered them to
govern him as they pleafed ; nay, though
broad hints were given that the chaplain
was an emiffary of lord Peter, and was taking advantage of the old lady's hyfterics to
bring the whole family into his intereft, John
gave no heed to any of thefe infinuations.

As foon as the letter of Peregrine Pickle
arrived, the apprentices, to whom it was
directed, held a confultation what they
fhould do. They were heartily tired of
the conduct of the chaplain ; they lamented the old lady's ill health, and wifhed for
a cure ; but there was at prefent no hope
of it, and they concluded that it was beft
to follow Pickle's advice, and retire with
him into the Foreft. Though they were
infected with the fpirit of adventure, yet
they

they were a fet of wary fellows, and knew
they could not with fafety venture thither
unlefs they had a leafe of the land.   Happily, however, for them, Bull had a little
while before that put the affairs of the Foreft into the hands of a gentleman of the
law,* with orders to fee that the matter
was properly managed, fo as to yield him
fome certain profit.   To this fage they applied, and for the proper fees, which they
clubbed for between them, they obtained a
leafe, under hand and feal; wherein, for
" fundry caufes him thereunto moving, the
faid Bull did grant and convey unto John
Codline and his affociates, fo many acres of
his Foreft, bounded fo and fo, and which
they were to have, hold, and enjoy for ever
and ever, yielding and paying fo and fo,
and fo forth."   When this grand point was
gained by the affiftance of the lawyer and
his clerks, who knew how to manage bufinefs, the adventurers fold all their fuper-
fluities to the pawn-brokers, and got together what things they fuppofed they
                                    fhould

* The Council of Plymouth in Devonfhire.

should want, and leaving behind them a note on the compter,* to tell their master where they were bound, and what were their defigns; they set off all together and got safe into a part of the Foreft adjoining to Pickle, who, hearing of their arrival, took his oaken ftaff in his hand, and hobbled along as faft as his lame legs could carry him to fee them, and a joyful meeting indeed they had. Having laid their heads together, it was agreed that Codline fhould fend for a girl whom he had courted,† and marry her, and that he fhould be confidered as the lord of the manor, that Pickle fhould have a leafe of that part which he had pitched upon, and that Ploughfhare and Carrier fhould for the prefent be confidered as members of Codline's family. John had taken a great fancy to fifhing, and thought he could wholly or chiefly fubfift by it; but Humphry had a mind for a farm; fo after a while they parted in friendfhip.

* Letter written on board the Arabella, after the embarkation of the Maffachufetts fettlers.

† The Maffachufetts charter.

friendſhip. Humphry, with a pack on his back and a ſpade in his hand, travelled a-croſs the Foreſt; till he found a wide mead-ow with a large brook* running through it, which he ſuppoſed to be within John's grant, and intended ſtill to conſider himſelf as a diſtant member of the family. But as it fell out otherwiſe, he was obliged to get a new leaſe, to which Mr. Frog made ſome objections, but they were over-ruled; and ſoon after another old fellow ſervant, THE-OPHILUS WHEAT-EAR, came and ſat down by him. They being ſo much alike in their views and diſpoſitions, agreed to live to-gether as intimates, though in two families, which they did till Wheat-ear's death, when Ploughſhare became his ſole heir, and the eſtate has ever ſince been his. This Hum-phry was always a very induſtrious, frugal, ſaving huſband; and his wife, though a formal ſtrait-laced ſort of a body, yet al-ways minded her ſpinning and knitting, and took excellent care of her dairy. She al-ways cloathed her children in homeſpun gar-
ments,

* Connecticut River.

ments, and fcarcely ever fpent a farthing
for outlandifh trinkets. The family and
all its concerns were under very exact reg-
ulations : not one of them was fuffered to
peep out of doors after the fun was fet.
It was never allowed to brew on Saturday,.
left the beer fhould break the Fourth Com-
mandment by working on Sunday : and
once, it is faid, the ftallion was impounded
a whole week for holding *crim. con.* with
the mare while the Old gentleman was at
his devotions. Bating thefe peculiarities,
(and every body has fome) Humphry was
a very good fort of a man, a kind neighbour,
very thriving, and made a refpectable figure. Though he lived a retired life, and
did not much follow the fafhions, yet he
raifed a good eftate, and brought up a large
family. His children and grand-children
have penetrated the interior parts of the
country, and feated themfelves on the beft
foil, which they know how to diftinguifh
at firft fight, and to cultivate to the greateft advantage. Whereever you find them,
you find good hufbandmen.

Letter III.

JOHN CODLINE *quarrels with* ROGER CAR-
RIER, *and turns him out of Doors.* CAR-
RIER *retires to another Part of the Forest.*
CODLINE *surveys his Land; takes* ROBERT
LUMBER *under his Protection*—*Begins a
Suit with the Fishermen of* LEWIS, *which,
with other Incidents, excites the Jealousy of
Mr.* BULL.

DEAR SIR,

AFTER Ploughshare's departure,
John Codline with his family kept on their
fishing and planting, and fometimes went
a hunting, fo that they made out to get a
tolerable fubfiftence. John's family grew,
and he fettled his fons as faft as they became of age, to live by themfelves; and
                                                        when

when any of his old acquaintance came to
fee him, he bade them welcome, and was
their very good friend, *as long as they continued to be of his mind*, and no longer ; for he
was a very pragmatical fort of a fellow,
and loved to have his own way in every
thing. This was the caufe of a quarrel
between him and *Roger Carrier*, for it happened that Roger had taken a fancy to dip
his head into water,* as the moft effectual
way of wafhing his face, and thought it
could not be made fo clean in any other
way. John, who ufed the common way of
taking water in his hand, to wafh his face,
was difpleafed with Roger's innovation,
and remonftrated againft it. The remonftrance had no other effect, than to fix
Roger's opinion more firmly ; and as a farther improvement on his new plan, he
pretended that no perfon ought to have his
face wafhed till he was capable of doing it
himfelf, without any affiftance from his
parents. John was out of patience with
this addition, and plumply told him, that
if

* Anabaptifts.

if he did not reform his principles and practice, he would fine him, or flog him, or kick him out of doors. These threats put Roger on inventing other odd and whimsical opinions. He took offence at the letter X, and would have had it expunged from the alphabet, because it was the shape of a crofs, and had a tendency to introduce Popery.* He would not do his duty at a military muster, because there was an X in the colours. After a while he began to scruple the lawfulnefs of bearing arms, and killing wild beasts. But, poor fellow! the worst of all was, that being feized with a shaking palfy,† which affected every limb and joint of him, his fpeech was fo altered that he was unable to pronounce certain letters and fyllables as he had been ufed to do. Thefe oddities and defects rendered him more and more difagreeable to his old friend, who, however, kept his temper as well as he could, till one day, as John was faying a long grace

---

* Roger Williams's zeal againft the fign of the crofs.
† Quakers.

grace over his meat, Roger kept his hat on the whole time.   As soon as the ceremony was over, John took up a cafe-knife from the table, and gave Roger a blow on the ear with the broad fide of it, then with a rifing ftroke turned off his hat. Roger faid nothing, but taking up his hat put it on again; at which John broke out into fuch a paffionate fpeech as this—"You impudent fcoundrel! is it come to this? Have I not borne with your whims and fidgets thefe many years, and yet they grow upon you ? Have I not talked with you time after time, and proved to you as plain as the nofe in your face that your no-tions are wrong ? Have I not ordered you to leave them off, and warned you of the confequence, and yet you have gone on from bad to worfe ? You began with dip-ping your head into water, and would have all the family do the fame, pretending there was no other way of wafhing the face. You would have had the children go dirty all their days, under pretence that they were not able to wafh their own faces,

and

and fo they muft have been as flithy as
the pigs till they were grown up. Then
you would talk your own balderdafh lin-
go, *thee and thou, and nan forfooth*—and
now you muft keep your hat on when I
am at my devotions, and I fuppofe would
be glad to have the whole family do the
fame ! There is no bearing with you any
longer—fo now, hear me, I give you fair
warning, if you don't mend your manners,
and retract your errors, and promife reformation, I'll kick you out of the houfe. I'll
have no fuch refractory fellows here : I
came into this foreft for *reformation*, and
reformation I *will* have."

" FRIEND John (faid Roger) doft not
thou remember when thou and I lived together in friend Bull's family, how hard
thou didft think it to be compelled to look
on thy book all the time that the hooded
chaplain was reading the prayers, and how
many knocks and thumps thou and I had
for offering to ufe our liberty, which we
thought we had a right to ? Didft thou

not

not come hitherunto for the fake of enjoy-
ing thy liberty, and did not I come to enjoy mine? Wherefore then doſt thou aſ-
ſume to deprive me of the right which
thou claimeſt for thyſelf?"

"DON'T tell me (anſwered John) of
right and of liberty—you have as much
liberty as any man ought to have. You
have liberty to do right, and no man ought
to have liberty to do wrong."

"WHO is to be judge (replied Roger)
of what is right or what is wrong? Ought
not I to judge for myſelf? or, Thinkeſt
thou it is thy place to judge for me?"

"WHO is to be judge? (ſaid John) why,
the book is to be judge; and I have proved
by the book over and over again that you
are wrong, and therefore you are wrong,
and you have no liberty to do any thing but
what is right."

.D   "BUT

- "But friend John, (said Roger) who is to judge whether thou hast proved my opinions or conduct to be wrong—thou or I ?"

"Come, come, (said John) not so close neither; none of your idle distinctions : I *say* you are in the wrong, I have *proved* it, and *you know* it; you have sinned against *your own conscience,* and therefore you deserve to be cut off as an incorrigible heretic."

"How dost thou know (said Roger) that I have sinned against my own conscience ? Canst thou search the heart ?"

At this John was so enraged that he gave him a smart kick on the posteriors, and bade him be gone out of his house, and off his lands, and called after him to tell him, that if ever he should catch him there again he would knock his brains out. Roger, having experienced the logic of the foot, applied to the seat of honour, walked off, with as much *meekness* as hu-

man

man nature is capable of, on such occa-
sions; and having travelled as far as he
supposed to be out of the limits of John's
lease, laid himself down by the side of a
clear rivulet, which flowed down a hill;
here he composed himself to sleep, and on
his awaking found several bears about him,
but none offered him any insult. Upon
which he said, and minuted it down in his
pocket-book, "Surely the beasts of the
wildernefs are in friendship with me, and
this is designed by *Providence** as my rest-
ing place; here, therefore, will I pitch my
tabernacle, and here shall I dwell more in
peace, though surrounded by bears and
wolves, than when in the midst of those
whom I counted my brethren."

On this spot he built an hut, and having
taken possession, made a visit to his old master Bull, who gave him a lease of the place,
with an island or two in an adjoining cove

D 2   of

* The town of Providence was built by emigrants
from Masfachusetts, of whom Roger Williams was
head.

of the great lake, and recommended to him a wife, by whom he had a few children; but his plantation was chiefly increased by the flocking of strangers to him; for he was a very hospitable man, and made it a rule in his family not to refuse any who should come, whether lame or blind, short or tall, whether they had two eyes or one, whether they squinted, or stammered, or limped, or had any other natural defect or impediment; it was another rule that all should bear with the infirmities of their neighbours, and help them as they were able. Once, as I was passing through Roger's plantation, I saw one man carrying another on his shoulders, which, at first, I thought a very odd sight; upon coming up to them, I perceived that the lower one was blind, and the upper one was lame, so as they had but one pair of eyes and one pair of legs between them, the lame man availed himself of the blind man's legs, and he of the other's eyes, and both went along very well together. I remember also, that as I passed along, the fences were in

some

some places made of very crooked, knotty rails; but the crooks and knots were made to say into each other so cleverly, that the fences were as tight as if they had been made of stuff sawed ever so even; a circumstance which convinced me that very crooked things might be put together, to advantage, if proper pains were taken.

WHEN John Codline had settled the controversy with Roger, by kicking him out of doors, he began to look about him to see what his neighbours were doing. Having found a young fellow on his north-eastern limits, who had come thither without his knowledge or permission, he took it into his head to survey the extent of his grounds. The words of his lease were rather ambiguous, and by virtue thereof, he thought it convenient to extend his claims over the lands on which *Robert Lumber* (for that was the name of the young fellow) had settled. It seems that Bob had been sent by some of John Bull's family to erect a fishing stage on the borders of

I   the

the lake, and the lawyer who had the care of the foreſt not being acquainted ſo much as he ought to have been with the ſituation of the lands, or having no knowledge of the art· of ſurveying, had made out a leaſe which lapped over Codline's ; ſo that each of them had a claim upon the ſame land. In ſome circumſtances this might have been deemed unfortunate, but as it happened it proved lucky for poor Bob. His employers had left him in the lurch, and he would have ſtarved to death if John had not taken him under his wing and ſent him proviſions to keep him alive. He alſo lent him a hand to clear up the buſhes, and furniſhed him with materials to build a ſaw-mill. This ſet Bob on his own legs, and he proved a ſturdy faithful fellow. He was of great ſervice to John in killing bears and wolves that infeſted his plantation ; and when he himſelf was in danger, John lent him powder, ſhot, and flints, and ſent hands to help him ; and in ſo doing he ſerved himſelf as well as his neighbour, which was no breach of morality. Thus they lived pretty peaceably

ably together, till after a while Bob's old
owners found the land was grown good for
something, and then (without paying John
for his affiftance in making it fo) appealed
to Mr. Bull, *and got it away*, and took a
large flice of John's land into the bargain.*
This was a matter which ftuck in John's
throat a great while, and if I am rightly informed he has hardly fwallowed it yet.
He did not think himfelf fairly dealt by,
though he had all Peregrine Pickle's land
put into a new leafe which Bull gave him.
To be fhort, John Codline and John Bull
never heartily loved one another; they
were in their temper and difpofition too
much alike; each was eternally jealous of
the other; and this jealoufy was kept alive
by a variety of incidents which it would be
too tedious to enumerate. One of them,
however, was of fo fingular a nature that
I think it deferves to be remembered. It
was this. Lewis had erected a fifhing
stage

* The fettling the line between Maffachufetts and
New Hampfhire.

ſtage and ware-houſe* on the northeaſt, which interfered with Codline's favourite employment. Without conſulting his old Maſter Bull, or waiting for his advice or orders, Jack ſent a bailiff with a writ of in-truſion to the fiſhermen, and began a ſuit in law. Mr. Bull hearing of it, was glad to take advantage of the circumſtance and fee council in the cauſe, which finally went in his favour. But though the iſſue of the cauſe was of ſo much advantage to him; yet he ever after looked upon Codline as a forward, meddling fellow, for running on that errand before he was ſent; and there were not wanting perſons who were con-tinually buzzing in his ear, to keep a good look out on that impudent jackanapes, or he would ſoon begin to think himſelf as good a man as his maſter.

* Louiſburg.

Letter IV.

Attempt of NICHOLAS FROG *and* GUSTAVUS *the Ironmonger, to intrude into the Forest.— Their quarrel.—Mr.* BULL's *Sickness and Delirium.—His Policy in paying his Debts. —His Quarrel with* FROG, *and its Termination by Compromise.—Plantation of* CART-RUT *and* BARE-CLAY, *called* CÆSAREA.—*Lease to* CHARLES INDIGO.

DEAR SIR,

IN my laft letter I had got a little too forward in my ftory, in point of time ; but as I write by piecemeal, and often in a hurry, you muft excufe chronological inaccuracy. I now go back to tell you, that between the lands occupied by Marygold, and thofe on which Ploughfhare had made

his

his fettlement, was a large tract of wafte, where none of Mr. Bull's family had ever been; but the report of the plantations which one and another of them had made, drew the attention of Bull's neighbours. Among thefe, *Nicholas Frog* was not an idle fpectator. He was as fly a fellow as you will meet with in a fummer's day, always attentive to his intereft, and never let flip an opportunity to promote it. Obferving that Mr. Bull was rather carelefs of the Foreft, and trufted his lawyers and fervants with the management of it, and knowing there was a large flice of it unoccupied, he clandeftinely fent out fome furveyors in the difguife of hunters, to make a defcription of the country, and report to him at their return. Another good neighbour, *Guftavus* the ironmonger, was gaping after. it, and gave out word among his journeymen, that if any of them would adventure thither and fet up their trade, he would uphold them in their pretenfions, and lend them any affiftance in his power. Accordingly one of them, by the name of *Cafimir*,
ventured.

ventured to make a beginning on the fhore
of a navigable creek ;* but did not care to
penetrate far into the country, on account
of the wolves and bears, which were very
numerous thereabout. As foon as Frog
heard of this, he picked a quarrel with
Guftavus, and infifted that the land was
his, by poffeffion, becaufe he had already
fent furveyors thither.   It happened, however, that the place which Frog's people
had pitched upon was at the mouth of another creek,† at a confiderable diftance;
where they had built a hut, on a point of
land, and farther up the creek had erected
a kind of lodge or hunting houfe,‡ for the
convenience of collecting game.   On this
plantation Frog had placed *Peter Stiver*, a
one-legged fellow, as his overfeer.   As
foon as Peter heard of the quarrel between
his mafter and Guftavus, he thought the
quickeft way of ending it was the beft;
and therefore, without waiting for orders
or ceremony, he went and commanded
Cafimir off the ground; and with one of

his

* The Delaware.   † Hudfon's river.   ‡ Albany.

his crutches beat his houfe to pieces about his ears. The poor fellow ftared at this rough treatment ; but was glad to efcape with whole bones, and humbly requefted leave to remain there with his tools, prom- ifing to follow his bufinefs quietly, and become an obedient fervant to Mr. Frog. Upon thefe conditions he was permitted to remain, and the whole tract was reputed Frog's property.

WHILE thefe things were doing, John Bull was confined to his houfe with a vio- lent fever and delirium, which ended in the hypochondria,* and his imagination was the feat of every wild freak and ftrange vagary. One while he fancied himfelf an abfolute monarch ; then, a prefbyterian clergyman ; then a general of horfe ; then a lord protector: His noddle was filled with a jumble of polemic divinity, political difputes, and military arrangements, and it was not till after much blood-letting, bliftering, vomiting, purging, cold-bathing, and

* The civil wars in England.

and horfe-trotting, that he began to mend. Under this fevere but wholefome regimen, he at length grew cool and came to himfelf, but found on his recovery that his affairs had gone behind hand during his ficknefs. Befide the lofs of bufinefs, he had phyficians' and apothecaries' bills to pay, and thofe who had attended upon him as nurfes, watchers, porters, &c. all expected wages or douceurs, and were continually haunting him with, "How does your honor do? I am glad to fee your honor fo well as to be abroad." They were continually putting themfelves in his way; and if they did not directly *dun* him for payment, their looks were fo fignificant that a man of lefs penetration could eafily have gueffed what was their meaning.

BULL was fomewhat perplexed how to anfwer all their demands and expectations. He was too far behind hand to be able to fatisfy them, and withal too generous to let them remain unpaid. At length he hit on this expedient : "Thefe fellows, faid

he

he to himfelf, have ferved me well, and may be of ufe to me again. There is yet a confiderable part of my foreft unoccupied. I'll offer to leafe them tracts of land which *coft me nothing*, and if they will accept them at a low rent, they may prove ufeful fervants, and I fhall be a gainer as well as they." Having come to this refolution, he began to inquire into the affairs of his foreft, and found that his neighbours had intruded upon his claim. Lewis had taken poffeffion at one end;* Lord Strut at the other;† Nicholas Frog in the middle,‡ and his own tenants had been quarrelling with their new neighbours, as well as among themfelves. "Hey-day! fays John, this will never do; I muft keep a good look out upon thefe dogs, or they will get the advantage of me." Away he goes to Frog, and begun to complain of the ill treatment which he had received. Frog, who had

no

---

* Canada, poffeffed by the French.

† Florida, poffeffed by the Spaniards.

‡ New Amfterdam and the New Netherlands, by the Dutch.

no mind either to quarrel, or to cry *peccavi*, like a fly, evaſive whore-ſon as he was, ſhrugged up his ſhoulders, diſowned what his ſervants had done, and ſaid, "he ſuppoſed they only meant to kill game, and did not intend to hold poſſeſſion." Bull was not to be put off ſo; his blood was up, and he determined to treat Frog's ſervants as they had treated Caſimir. So, calling a truſty old ſtud out of his compting houſe, "Here Bob,* ſaid he, take one of my hunters with a pair of blood-hounds, and go to that part of the foreſt where Peter Stiver has encroached, give him fair warning; tell him the land is mine, and I will have it; if he gives up at once, treat him well, and tell him I'll give him leave to remain there; but if he offers to make any reſiſtance, or heſitates about an anſwer, ſet your dogs at him and drive him off; kill his cattle, and ſet his houſe on fire: Never fear, I'll bear you out in it." Away goes Bob, and delivered his meſſage.

Peter

* Sir Robert Carr's expedition againſt New Amſterdam, now New York.

Peter at firſt thought it a matter of amuſement, and began to divert himſelf with it; but as ſoon as the dogs opened upon him, he found his miſtake, and rather than run the riſk of being driven off, he quietly ſubmitted to the conditions propoſed. "Hang it, ſaid he to himſelf, what care I who is my landlord? Gain is my object; I have already been at great expenſe, and have a proſpect of getting an eſtate. To remove will ruin me; I'll therefore ſtay here, and make money under Bull, or Frog, or any other maſter that will let me ſtay."

In a ſubſequent quarrel which happened between Bull and Frog, the latter ſeized upon this plantation again, and Peter recognized his old maſter; but upon a compromiſe it was given up to Bull in exchange for a tract of ſwamp* which lay far to the ſouthward. Peter continued on the ground through all theſe changes, and followed his buſineſs with great diligence, collecting game and pelts, and vending them ſometimes

* Surrinam.

times to Mr. Bull, and sometimes to Mr. Frog. However, Bull thought it best, that in token of subjection, he should change his name; to which he consented, and partly to please his new master, and partly to retain the remembrance of his old one, he dropped the name of *Stiver*, and assumed the name of *Bullfrog*.

THE whole tract which was thus gotten from Frog, was thought too large for one plantation, and therefore Mr. Bull, in pursuance of the plan which he had formed, appropriated the rents of the plantation, on which Bullfrog was seated, to his brother,* and the other was leased to two of his servants, CART-RUT and BARE-CLAY, and some time after another tract was set off to WILLIAM BROADBRIM, whose father had been an assiduous rat-catcher in Bull's family; but more of this hereafter.

CART-RUT and *Bare-clay* agreed to divide their land into two farms, which they called

E

* Duke of York.

ed the eaft and weft farms; but when they
came to run the divifion line, their com-
paffes differed fo much that they could not
fix the boundary. This was one caufe of
diffention. Another was the different humours and difpofitions of their families.
Thofe on the eaft farm were brought up
under Mr. Bull's fifter PEG, and as it is
well known that fhe and her brother had
long been at variance, fo their domeftics
had got tinctured with the notions and prejudices of their refpective families. The
family on the weft farm was made up of
perfons who were fubject to the epidemic
ague or fhaking palfy;* with fome ftragglers from Bullfrog's and Cafimir's families.
From this diverfity of conftitutions and humours arofe bickerings and quarrels, a dif-
inclination to work and fubmit to family
government. Thefe diforders continued a
long while, and bufinefs went on very flow-
ly, till at length the heads of both families
agreed to give up their feparate leafes, and
take a new one of the whole, and let Mr.
Bull

* The Quakers.

Bull appoint an overseer. By these means peace was restored, and the new overseer, who was supposed to be a descendant of a natural son of JULIUS CÆSAR, gave the name of his ancestor to the farm, which has ever since been called CÆSAREA.

THERE was another portion of the forest, which lay southward of Walter Pipeweed's plantation, and which no person had yet taken up, though some had made attempts and had been driven off by the numberless musquetoes and sand-flies, which abound in those places. Mr. Bull was still desirous to reward his friends in the *cheapest manner*, and at the same time to keep his neighbours from encroaching upon him, and secure the possession of the forest to himself. In pursuance of his plan, and to make short work of it at once, he leased the whole of this southern extremity to CHARLES INDIGO, who was expressly ordered to take under his care and into his family all persons who had attended Mr. Bull, in his late sickness, in quality of nurses,

E 2   druggists,

druggifts, apothecaries, laundreffes, uphol-
fters, porters, watchers, &c. &c. By this
order Charles found himfelf at once fur-
rounded by a large body of retainers of
various ranks and qualities, and, being a
fpeculator himfelf, he employed a fpecula-
tive man, Mr. *Padlock*, who had written a
large treatife upon *Ideas*, to draw up fome
rules, for the management of fuch a family, intending when he fhould build an
houfe, to pafte it up in the parlour, as a di-
rectory to his wife. Accordingly Mr. Padlock went to work, and with an exquifite
mixture of political and metaphyfical knowledge, diftinguifhed between the hall, the parlour, the dreffing-room, the gallery, the mu-
fic-room, the bed-chambers, the chapel,
the kitchen, the water-clofet, &c. fhewing
what was to be done in each, and the proper fubordination of one to the other, all
which would have been of excellent fervice
in a palace, and among people who had got
to a high degree of refinement, but was ill
fuited to the circumftances of new adventurers

turers in a foreft. They rather needed to
be inftructed in the method of felling trees,
draining fwamps, digging clams, guard-
ing againft mufquetoes, killing wolves and
bears, and erecting huts to keep off the
weather. To thefe neceffary affairs they
were obliged to attend, and Mr. Padlock's
fine fpun rules were laid by and little
thought of.

CHARLES had pitched upon a fandy.
point, between two brooks, for his manfion
houfe, and had made a fmall beginning,
when his repofe was difturbed by one Au-
GUSTINE, a lubberly fellow, who had taken
a leafe of Lord Strut, and lived farther
fouthward. This Strut was the largeft
landholder in the country, and was never
fatisfied with adding field to field. He had
already got much more than he could manage, and had greatly impoverifhed his
homeftead by attending to his extra territo-
ries. His tenants were infected with the
fame land fever, and wifhed to have no
neighbour within fight or call. With this
envious

envious difpofition, Auguftine collected a
rabble of loufy fellows, and was coming to
difpoffefs Charles, thinking him too weak
to make a defence; but Charles was a lad
of too much *fpunk* to be brow-beaten. He
armed all his people with fome weapon or
other, and advanced till he came within fight of the place where Auguftine was,
who, on feeing him, took wit in his anger,
and went back, without attempting any
mifchief.

ANOTHER difficulty which Charles expected to encounter was from the wild
beafts ; but luckily for him, thefe creatures
got into a quarrel among themfelves, and
fought with each other till they had thin-
ned their numbers confiderably, fo that
Charles and his companions could venture
into the woods, where they caught fome
few and tamed them, as was the ufual practice among all Mr. Bull's tenants at that
day.   Of this practice a more particular account fhall be given in my next letter.

Letter V.

Mr. BULL's *Project of taming wild Animals.*
—Its Execution by his Tenants.—Their different Notions and Conduct in this Matter.

DEAR SIR,

Y OU muſt have remarked in your acquaintance with the life and character of Mr. John Bull, that he is very whimſical, and as poſitive as whimſical. Among oth-. er advantages which he expected from the ſettlement of his Foreſt, one was, that the wild animals, whom nature had made ferocious and untractable in the higheſt degree, would be rendered tame and ſerviceable, by receiving inſtruction and education from the nurturing hand of humanity. He had conceived a notion that every creature has certain

latent

latent principles and qualities which form a foundation for improvement ; and he thought it a great piece of injuſtice that theſe qualities ſhould be ſuffered to remain uncultivated : he had a mind that experiments ſhould be attempted to diſcover how far this kind of cultivation was practicable, and what uſe could be made of the animal powers under the direction and control of rational government. Full of this idea, he came to a reſolution, that it ſhould be the duty of every one of his tenants to catch wild beaſts of various ſorts, and diſcipline them ſo as to find out their ſeveral properties and capacities, and uſe them accordingly ; and this kind of ſervice was mentioned in their reſpective leaſes as one condition of the grants.

Some of the tenants, particularly Peregrine Pickle, John Codline, and Humphry, Ploughſhare, entered zealouſly into the meaſure from principle. They had, during Mr. Bull's ſickneſs and delirium, before ſpoken of, formed an aſſociation for their mutual ſafety.

fafety.* The object of their union was two fold: firft, to endeavour by all fair means to tame and difcipline the wild beafts; and fecondly, in cafe of their proving refractory, to defend themfelves againft their attacks. The other tenants did fomething in the fame way; fome from one principle, and fome from another. Peter Bullfrog, who was as cunning as any of them, made ufe of thofe which he had tamed, as his caterers, to provide game for his table, of which the feathers and furs ferved him as articles of traffic, and brought him in a profitable return.

THE principal confideration (fetting afide intereft) which induced the more zealous of the Forefters to enter into this bufinefs, was an idea that thefe animals were a degenerated part of the human fpecies, and might be reftored to their proper rank and order, if due pains were taken. The grounds of this opinion were thefe: Among the traditions of the ancient Druids there was a ftory,

* The united colonies of New England, 1643.

a ſtory, that out of *twelve* families which
inhabited a certain diſtrict by themſelves,
ten had been loſt, and no account could be
given of them ; and, where, ſaid they, is it
more likely to find them than in this foreſt,
in the ſhape of ſome other creatures ? eſpecially, if the doctrine of TRANSMIGRATION,
which the Druids held, be true. Another
tradition was, that one of Mr. Bull's great-
great-uncles, by the name of *Madok*, had
many years ago diſappeared, and the laſt
account which had been received of him
was, that he had been ſeen going towards
this foreſt ; hence it was concluded that his
deſcendants muſt be found here. In con-
firmation of this argument, it was alleged,
that the ſounds which ſome of theſe creatures made in their howlings, reſembled the
language ſpoken in that day : nay, ſome
were poſitive that they had heard them pronounce the word *Madokawando* ;* and one
hunter roundly ſwore that he had ſeen
in the den of a bear, an old *book* which he
ſuppoſed to be a *Bible* written in the Celtic
language,

* The name of a Sachem, at Penobſcot.

language, and this book they concluded muft have been left there by *Madok*, who could read and fpeak no other language. Another very material circumftance was the difcovery of a rock by the fide of a brook,* infcribed with fome characters which bore no refemblance to any kind of writing, ancient or modern ; the conclufion from hence was, that it muft be of the remoteft antiquity : this rock was deemed an unaccountable curiofity, till a certain virtuofo took it into his noddle, firft to imagine, and then to become extremely pofitive that the characters were *Punic* ; and finally this infcription was tranflated, and affirmed to be nothing lefs than a treaty of alliance and commerce between the *Phenicians* and the firft inhabitants of this foreft. From all thefe premifes it was inferred, with fome plaufibility, and more pofitivenefs, that one fpecies at leaft of the favage animals was defcended from *Madok*, and that the others were the pofterity of the long loft *ten* families, who were well known to have had a commercial

---

* The celebrated rock at Dighton, in Maffachufetts.

commercial connexion with the *Phenicians*, and that thefe probably found out their haunt, and followed them for the fake of their former friendfhip.———What happy light do modern difcoveries and conjectures throw on the dark pages of antiquity.

FROM thefe principles,. as well as from motives of humanity and of intereft, fome of the Forefters entered with zeal on the confideration and practice of the beft meth-ods to fulfil this condition of their grants, the difciplining of the favage animals, and they certainly deferve praife for their honeft endeavours ; but, others who pretended to the fame zeal, it is to be lamented, made ufe of this pretence to cover their vanity or their avarice. Had none but gentle means been ufed, it is probable more good might, on the whole, have been produced ; but as it often happens that many a good project has been ruined for want of pru-dence in the execution, fo it fared with this ; for while the new comers were bufy in putting up their huts, and preparing the land

land for cultivation, both of which were necessary before they could attend to any other business, some of the savage tribe would be a little impertinent, either by peeping into the huts, or breaking up a nest where the poultry were hatching, or carrying off a chick or a gosling.   These impertinencies bred frequent quarrels, and the poor creatures were sometimes driven off with bloody noses, or obliged to hop on three legs, or even laid sprawling and slyly covered with earth, no service or ceremony being said over the carcass, and no other epitaph, than " Poh, they are nothing but brutes, and where's the harm of killing them !" or in rhyme thus :

" Tit for tat, tit for tat,
" He stole my chick, and I broke his back."

WHATEVER plausible excuses might have been made for these proceedings, they served to render the creatures jealous of their new neighbours ; but instead of abating their appetite for mischief, it sharpened their invention to take more sly methods of
accomplishing

accomplishing it. The more wary of them kept aloof in the day time, and would not be enticed by the arts which were used to draw them in ; however, they were some-times pinched for food, and the new inhab-itants used to throw crusts of bread, hand-fuls of corn, and other eatables, in their way, which allured them by degrees to familiarity. After a while it was found that nothing succeeded so well as *molasses.* It was therefore thought a capital manœu-vre to drop a train of it on the ground, which the creatures would follow, licking it, till they had insensibly got up to the doors of the houses, where if any body held a bowl or a plate besmeared with the liquor, they would come and put their noses into it, and then you might pat them on the back and sides, or stroke them, say-ing, "Poor Bruin, poor Isgrim, poor Rey-nard, poor Puss," and the like, and they would suffer themselves to be handled and fondled till they dropped asleep. When they awaked, they would make a moan and wag their tails, as if they were asking for
more,

more, and if it was denied them, they would retire to the woods in difguſt, till the ſcent of the molaſſes operating on their depraved appetites, invited them to return where it was to be had.. This was, upon repeated trial, found to be the moſt effectual way of taming them, as they might be taught to imitate any kind of tricks and geſtures, if a diſh of molaſſes was held out as a reward..

THE Foreſters knew that they could not ingratiate themſelves better with their old maſter Bull, than by humouring his itch for projects. They therefore took care to raiſe reports and write letters from time to time concerning the wonderful ſucceſs which they had met with in civilizing the ſavage animals. Bull was greatly pleaſed with theſe reports, and made a practice of ſending preſents of trinkets to be diſtributed among them ; ſuch as collars, ear-rings, and noſe-jewels. Several times ſome of the moſt ſtately and beſt inſtructed of them were carried to his houſe for a ſhow, where

he

he had them dreſſed up in ſcarlet and gold
trappings, and led through all his apartments for the entertainment of his family,
and feaſted with every nick-nack which his
cook and confectioner could procure. He
was ſo fond of being thought their patron
and protector, that he uſually ſpoke of them
as his *red children*, from the colour of their
hides. It is not many years ſince one of
them, after being led through ſeveral families and plantations of the tenants, was
carried by a certain *witty cur*, to Mr. Bull's
own houſe, dreſſed in the habit of a *clergyman*, having been previouſly taught to lift
his paws and roll his eyes, as if in the act
of devotion. This trick was ſo well carried
on, that the managers of it picked up a large
pocket full of pence, by exhibiting him for
a raree-ſhow, and the money was applied
toward building a *menagerie*, to which beaſts
of all kinds might be brought and tamed.
This project, like many ſuch whims, has
made more noiſe than profit ; for moſt of
thoſe who were ſuppoſed to be tamed and
domeſticated, after they had been ſent back

to

to their native woods, with a view to their being inftrumental in taming their fellow favages, have returned to their former ferocious habits, and fome of them have proved greater rogues than ever, and have done more mifchief than they could otherwife have been capable of.

MR. Bull himfelf was once fo full of the project, that he got his chaplain and fome others to form themfelves into a club; the profeffed object of which was, to *propagate knowledge* among thefe favage creatures. After fome trials, which did not anfwer expectation, old Madam Bull conceived that the money which was collected might as well be expended in teaching Mr. Bull's own tenants themfelves a little better manners; for fome of them were rather awkward and flovenly in their deportment, while others were decent and devout *in their own way.* Madam, as we have before obferved, was a great zealot in the caufe of *uniformity,* and had a vaft influence over her fon, by virtue of which, the attention of

F   the

the club was principally directed to the promoting of this grand object. Accordingly, every one of the tenants was furnished with a Bible and a Prayer Book, a clean napkin, bafon, platter, and chalice, with a few devotional tracts, and fome young adventurers who had been educated in the family, were recommended as chaplains; who had alfo by-orders to keep a look out toward the favage animals, when they fhould fall in their way.

THE chaplains were tolerably well received in moft of the families; but fome, particularly Codline and Ploughfhare, who gloried in being able to fay their prayers *without book*, always looked four upon them, and would frequently fay to them, " Go, take care of the favage objects of your miffion, and don't come here to teach us, till you have learned better yourfelves." The chaplains in difguft, and perhaps in revenge, (for they were but men of like paffions) would pout and fwell and call *fchifmatie* and other canonical nick-names, of which there

is

is extant a large vocabulary, and would frequently write letters, much to the difadvantage of their opponents. It is not many
years fince they, with the club which fent
them, were pretty feverely handled by one
of Codline's own chaplains,* and it is fuppofed that they have ever fince been more
modeft ; certain it is, that they are now on
better terms with their neighbours than
formerly ; this may, in part, be owing to
Mr. Bull's deferting them and refufing to
pay them for their fervices ever fince the
time that he began to quarrel with his tenants. On that occafion fome of them removed their quarters ; others kept their old
places, and have got along as well as they
could without the help which they formerly
received.

* Dr. M—y—w.

F 2

Letter VI.

Adventures of CHARLES INDIGO *and* PETER
PITCH.——*Character of* WILLIAM BROAD-
BRIM.——*His Projects, Principles, and a
Specimen of his Harangues.*

DEAR SIR,

I HAVE obferved in a former letter, that the leafe which Mr. Bull gave to
Charles Indigo, obliged him to receive into
his family all fuch perfons as had been attendants on Mr. Bull during his ficknefs,
and for whom he had no other means of
providing. This general indulgence procured to Charles the reputation of a very
friendly, hofpitable perfon, and induced
great numbers of other people of various
characters, views, and interefts, to feek an
afylum

afylum within his limits.   About this time
Mr. Lewis had grown fick and peevifh, and
had feverely cudgelled fome of his apprentices, becaufe they did not make their P's
and Q's exactly to his mind.* 'The poor
fellows, to prevent worfe treatment, fled
from his houfe, and took refuge with Mr.
Bull, who treated them civilly, and recommended them to the Foreft, where they
difperfed themfelves in the feveral families
of his tenants, and a large party of them
took up their abode with Charles, to whom
they proved an induftrious, profitable ac-
quifition, though fome of the family looked
a little fourly upon them.

THIS facility of admitting ftrangers produced an effect which had almoft proved
fatal to the reputation of the family; for a
number of *highwaymen* alfo fought fhelter
there, and by means of their gold and filver,
which they had in plenty, made friends
in the houfe, and were admitted by night
at

* Revocation of the edict of Nantz, by Lewis XIV.
1685.

at a back door. After a while they grew more bold, and came in the day time, under the difguife of pedlars, with packs on their fhoulders. One of them actually took his ftand behind a corner of one of the fences, from whence he fallied out on travellers; this corner obtained, from that circumftance, the name of *Cape Fear*; and as the firft names of places are not eafily got rid of, it retains the name to this day, and perhaps will ever retain it. Here the rafcal intended to have built himfelf a lodge, and taken up his quarters for life; but the matter was now grown fo public, that Charles, for the honour of his family, ordered all ftragglers to be feized, and this fellow in particular, after a fevere ftruggle, was apprehended and brought to juftice.

THE fame fpot was afterward taken poffeffion of by PETER PITCH, a poor fellow who got his living as he did his name, from collecting the refinous juice of the numerous pines which grew thereabout.

He

He had to work hard and fare hard, and go a great way for his victuals and clothes; but after he had lived alone for some time, he picked up one or two acquaintances of his own stamp, and they formed a family, which was at first rather disorderly. Farther discovery of the lands, and the advantage of the water carriage, induced some other people to sit down by him, and in process of time he became so respectable as to be noticed by Mr. Bull, who, though he never gave him a lease in form, yet let him have cloth and haberdashery upon credit, and took his pitch in payment as fast as he could collect it. This kept him in a dependent state, and subjected him to impositions from Bull's clerks and journeymen. About five and twenty years ago, Bull sent him a taylor to *try on* a new coat,* which was so strait that it split in several places, and never could be altered so as to fit him; but he was obliged to wear it, rather than quarrel with his patron. This same taylor was remarkable for *cabbaging*,

as

* Insurrections in North Carolina, 1771.

as Peter Bullfrog and Humphry Plough-
fliare have fince had large experience.

To finifh what relates to Charles Indigo,
I fhall obferve, that the land on which he
began his plantation, was in general fo wet
and miry, that it was unfavourable to the
production of wheat, and it was for fome
time doubtful whether he would be able to
raife his own bread.   Chance at length
effected what labour and ingenuity could
not : a bird of paffage having dropped
fome kernels of rice in his dung, it was
found to thrive exceedingly well ; from
whence the hint was taken, and rice became
the ftandard grain of the plantation.   By
the cultivation of this, and of a weed which
was ufeful to the dyers, he grew rich, and
made a fightly figure among his neighbours
in point of drefs and equipage ; though
his countenance is rather fallow, and he is
fubject to frequent returns of the inter-
mittent fever.

By

' By the extensive leafe given to Indigo and his affociates, moft of Mr. Bull's dependants and attendants were provided for, and their fervices recompenfed with a fhew of generofity on his part, and of fatisfaction on theirs. I have before juft hinted at a grant made to WILLIAM BROADBRIM, of which I fhall now give a more particular account.

His father had been an old fervant of Mr. Bull, and had been employed in the very laborious and neceffary bufinefs of catching and killing rats. In this employment he was fo very dexterous and fuccefsful, that he recommended himfelf highly to his mafter, who not only allowed him large wages, but promifed him farther recompenfe. During Mr. Bull's ficknefs, the care and diligence of this faithful fervant had been unremitted, and his merits were thereby increafed, fo that Mr. Bull, on his recovery, found himfelf deeply indebted to him, and he ftill continued his fervices ; till, worn out with age and infirmity,

firmity, he died and had an honourable funeral.

His son William then became his heir, and folicited for payment of the arrears due to his father, which Mr. Bull, according to the maxim he had laid down for himfelf, and urged by the neceffity of the occafion, propofed to difcharge by a leafe of part of the Foreft. This happened to fall in, exactly, with William's views, which were of a fingular nature.

About this time a nervous diforder appeared in Bull's family, which went by the name of the *fhaking palfy.** We fhall not pretend to trace the caufes of it, as the origin of fuch things is often obfcure and impenetrable ; but the effects were, a trembling of the nerves, a ftiffnefs in the neck and fhoulders, and a hefitancy in the fpeech, fo that it was impoffible for the patients to incline the head, or pronounce certain words and fyllables, fuch as Sir, Madam,

* Quakerifm.

Madam, your Honor, my Lord, &c. nor
could one of them raife his hand to take off
his hat, or hold it on the book when an·
oath was to be adminiftered.

Mr. Bull's choleric temper mifinter-
preted this natural infirmity into a fullen·
difrefpect. When he found a change in
the behaviour of thefe domeftics; that inftead of bowing to him they ftood upright
as a may-pole, and inftead of Sir, and your
Honor, they could utter nothing but *Friend,*
he grew angry, and made a pretty free ufe
of his fift; and when he found that they
could not be cured by fuch means, he thruft
fome of them into a dark clofet, and fhut
them up till they fhould, as he termed it,
"learn better manners;" and it is fuppofed he would have carried his refentment
much further, but for this circumftance :
William Broadbrim, who had himfelf ftrong
fymptoms of the diforder, whifpered to
Mr. Bull, that if he would give him time
to ripen a project, which he had conceived,
he would rid him of all trouble with thefe
people.

people. William had a plodding genius, and the fcheme with which his head was pregnant at this time, was nothing more or lefs than to make a fettlement in the foreft, and take all thefe people with him. Bull, who was glad to get rid of them, and of the debt which he owed to William, readily fell in with the project; and a grant was made out under hand and feal, wherein William Broadbrim, and his heirs, were invefted with the right of foil, and all other privileges of proprietorfhip, in a certain part of the foreft, between the plantation of Marygold and that of Cart-rut and Bareelay, being in the neighbourhood of the fpot where Cafimir had rebuilt his hut, and lived in an ambiguous fituation, not knowing who was his landlord. With him William made a peaceable compromife, faying, " Friend, I will do thee no violence, there is room enough for us both." Cafimir was glad of fo good a neighbour, and he had reafon to be, for he throve more rapidly after this than before.

WILLIAM

WILLIAM pitched upon a level piece of ground, where two large brooks met, for the fituation of his manfion houfe, and went to work to draw up rules for the government of his family. One of which was, that no perfon fhould be refufed admittance into it, or difturbed in it, or caft out of it, on account of any natural infirmity. Another was, that no arms nor ammunition fhould ever be made ufe of, on any pretence whatever. The firft of thefe rules gained William great reputation among all fenfible men ; the latter was a notion which candor would lead us to fuppofe procceded from a love of peace, and the exercife of good will toward his fellow-creatures; though fome were fo ill-natured as to imagine that it was an effect of the diforder in his nerves.

WHEN any of William's neighbours, who were of a different way of thinking, fpake to him of the impolicy of this rule, and afked him how he expected to defend himfelf and his family againft the wild beafts, if they fhould attack him ; William, who was

fond

fond of harangue, would anfwer thus—
"There is in all creatures a certain inftinct, which difpofeth them to peace. This
inftinct is fo ftrong and fixed, that upon it,
as upon a foundation, may be erected a
complete fyftem of love and concord, which
all the powers of anarchy fhall not be able
to overthrow. To cultivate and improve
this inftinct, is the bufinefs of every wife
man, and he may reafonably expect that an
example of this kind, if fteadily and regularly adhered to, will have a very extenfive
and beneficial influence, on all forts of
creatures; even the wild beafts of the foreft will become tame as lambs, and birds of
prey harmlefs as doves. Doft thou not fee,
friend, what influence my example has
already had on thofe creatures which are
deemed favage ? I go into their dens with
fafety, and they enter my habitation without
fear. When they are hungry I feed them,
when they are thirfty I give them drink,
and they in return bear my burdens, and
do fuch other kind offices as they are capable of, and I require of them. I have even
tamed

tamed fome of them fo far, that they have
fold me the land on which they live, and
have acknowledged the bargain by a mark
made with their toe-nails on parchment.
They are certainly fome of the beft natured
creatures in the world ; their native inftinct
leads them to love and peace, and fociabil-
ity ; and as long as I fet them a good example, I have no doubt they will follow it.
When fuch is my opinion and expectation,
why fhould I be anxious about what may,
and I truft never will happen ? Why fhould
I put myfelf in a pofture of defence againft
thofe who may never attack me ? or, why
fhould I, by the appearance of jealoufy and
diftruft on my part, offend thofe who now put
confidence in me ? No, no, I will not fuppofe that they will ever hurt me. I will not
fuffer the *carnal weapon* to be feen in my
houfe, nor fhall one of my family ever learn
the deteftable practice of pulling the *trigger*.
I leave the inftruments of deftruction to
the offspring of Cain and the feed of the
ferpent ; whilft I meekly imitate the gen-
tlenefs

tlenefs of the lamb, and the innocence of
the dove."

WITH fuch harangues William would
frequently entertain himfelf and his friends,
and he was fo fanguine in his benevolent
projeƈt, that inftead of having his own name,
as was ufual, written over his door, he had
the words BROTHERLY LOVE, tranflated into the Greek language, ΦΙΛΑΔΕΛΦΙΑ, and
infcribed in golden characters, as a ftanding invitation to perfons of all nations and
characters, to come and take fhelter under
his roof.

Letter VII.

Diffenfions in BROADBRIM's *Family.—His Averfion to Fire-Arms and its Confequence. Mr.* BULL's *fecond Sicknefs, and fecond Marriage.—His Project for making a new Plantation.—The Care of it committed to* GEORGE TRUSTY.—*Trout Fifhery eftablifhed at the Plantation of* ALEXANDER SCOTUS.

DEAR SIR,

THE general invitation which William Broadbrim had given to all perfons who were deftitute of a home, to come and take fhelter under his roof, and the gentle, humane treatment which thofe who accepted the invitation met with, fpread his fame abroad, and brought him much company. His family was fometimes com-

G pared

pared to the Ark of Noah, becaufe there was fcarcely any kind of being, of whatever fhape, fize, complexion, difpofition, or language, but what might be found there. He had alfo the art to keep them pretty well employed. Induftry, frugality, and temperance, were the leading principles of his family ; and their thriving was in a ratio compounded of thefe three forces. Nothing was wanting to make them as happy a family as any in the world, but a difpofition *among themfelves*, to live in peace. Unluckily, this defirable bleffing, on account of the variety of their humours and interefts, was feldom found among them. Ambition, jealoufy, avarice, and party fpirit, had frequent out-breakings, and were with difficulty quelled. It is needlefs to enter into a very particular difcuffion of the grounds or effects of thefe diffenfions : family quarrels are not very entertaining either at home or abroad, unlefs to fuch as delight in fcandal. But there was one caufe of diffenfion which it would be improper not to notice, becaufe I have already

hinted

hinted at the principle from which it proceeded. William's averfion to fire-arms was fo ftrong, that he would not fuffer any of his family to moleft the wild inhabitants of the foreft, though they were ever fo mifchievous. While the family was fmall, the favage animals who lived in the neighbourhood, being well fed, were tolerably tame and civil, but when the increafed number of the family had penetrated farther into the foreft, the haunts of the natives were difturbed, and the ftraggling labourers were fometimes furprifed, and having nothing to defend themfelves with, fell a facrifice to favage refentment. Remonftrances were prefented to Mr. Broadbrim one after another, but he always infifted on it that the fufferer muft have been the aggreffor, and that " they who take the fword, muft expect to perifh by the fword." At length the dead corpfe of one of the labourers, mangled and torn in a dreadful manner, was brought and laid at the door of William's parlour,* with a label affixed

G 2   to

* State houfe, 1755.

to the breaſt, on which were written theſe
words, " Thou thyſelf muſt be accounted
my murderer, becauſe thou didſt deny me
the means of defence." At ſight of this
horrid ſpectacle, Broadbrim turned pale !
the eye of his mind looked inward ! Nature
began to plead her own cauſe within him !
he gave way in ſome degree to her operations, though contrary to his pre-conceived
opinion, and with a trembling hand ſigned
a permiſſion for thoſe to uſe the *carnal
weapon*,* who could do it without ſcruple ;
and when they aſked him for money to
buy guns, powder and ball, he gave them
a certain ſum to provide *the neceſſaries of
life*, leaving them to put their own con-
ſtruction on the words. By degrees his
ſqueamiſhneſs decreaſed, and though it is
imagined he has ſtill ſome remainder of it,
yet neceſſity has ſo often overcome it, that
there is not much ſaid on the ſubject, un-
leſs it be very privately and among *friends*.
DURING

* Militia act.

DURING the time of which we have been
fpeaking, Mr. John Bull had undergone
another ficknefs,* not fo long nor fo violent
as the former, but much more beneficial in
its effects.   His new phyficians had adminiftered medicines which compofed his
nerves ; he ate, drank, and flept more regularly ; and he was advifed to marry again,
for his former wife had died of a confump-
tion a little before this ficknefs came on.
By thefe means his vigour was renewed,
but ftill his whimfical difpofition remained,
and broke out on feveral occafions.   When
he viewed his extenfive foreft, now planted
and thriving, under the honeft hand of induftry, he thought within himfelf that ftill
greater advantages might be derived from
that territory.   There was yet a part of it
unfettled between the plantation of Charles
Indigo, and the dominions of Lord Strut ;
and Bull thought it a pity to let fo much
remain a wildernefs.   The other plantations
had been made by difcontented fervants
and needy adventurers, who, ftruggling
with

* The Revolution, 1688.

with hardſhips, by a ſteady perſeverance had
ſurmounted many difficulties, and obtained
a comfortable living. "Now, ſaid Bull, if
theſe fellows have done ſo well, and got ſo
far aforehand, without having any capital of
their own to begin with, what cannot be
done by the force of my great capital? If
they have performed ſuch wonders, what
greater wonders may be brought into view
by my own exertions, with all the advantages
which it is in my power to command? To
it, boys; I vow I'll have a farm of my own
that ſhall beat you all!"—Having hit upon
this project, his brains immediately became
pregnant with ideas; but according to the
rule which he had lately preſcribed to himſelf, he communicated the matter to his
wife.　This good lady was not free from
an ambitious turn of mind.　She was extremely fond of having it thought that ſhe
had great influence over her huſband, and
would ſometimes gratify his humour at the
expenſe of her own judgment, rather than
not keep up this idea.　His expectations
from his new project were very ſanguine.

The

The land on which he had caft his eye was enough for a large farm; it had a fouthern expofure; it was warm, rich and fertile in fome parts, and in others boggy or fandy. He had converfed with fome foreigners, who told him that it was proper for the cultivation of wine and filk, and he imagined that if he could but add thefe articles to the lift of his own productions, there would be a great faving in the family. Mrs. Bull too was pleafed with the idea of having her filk gowns and ribbands of her own growth, and with the expectation of having the vaults filled with wine, made on her own plantation; for thefe and other good reafons, her thereunto moving, Madam gave her confent to the project. The perfon appointed to carry it into execution was *George Trufty*, a fenfible well bred merchant; but one who had only fpeculated in the fcience of agriculture, and knew nothing of it by experience. Having collected a number of poor people who were out of employment, he fent them to the fpot, with ftrict orders to work fix days in feven,

to

to keep their tools free from ruft, and their fire-arms in readinefs for their defence. Whatever they fhould earn was to be *their own* as long as they lived, and after their death their poffeffions were to defcend to their *fons*, and in default of male iffue to revert to the original grantor. They were not allowed to ufe black cattle in the labour of the field ; and were exprefsly forbidden to drink grog. Their bufinefs was to cultivate vines and mulberry trees, and to manufacture wine and filk. Upon this project another was grafted by the very fagacious *Doctor Squintum*, who chofe this new plantation as the moft convenient fpot in the world for a charity fchool, where *Orphans* might receive the beft education, and be fitted to be the pillars of church and State.

BUT notwithftanding the fums which Bull fo freely lavifhed out of his bags for the fupport of the vine and mulberry plantations ; and notwithftanding the collections which Squintum made among his numerous

ous devotees, thefe projects were either fo impracticable in themfelves, or fo ill conducted in the execution, that neither of them anfwered the expectations of the projectors. For want of black cattle, the foil could not be properly tilled; and for want of grog, the labourers fainted at their work; the right of inheritance being limited to the male line, women and girls were not fond of living there, and the men could not well live without them; land, cattle, women, and grog, were to be had elfewhere, and who would be confined to fuch a place? The land, too, was claimed by Lord Strut, who fent them writs of ejectment. As to the charity fchool, it was on trial found that the coft was more than the profit, and the building, which had fwallowed up thoufands of charity money, was finally confumed by fire. Poor George Trufty was difcouraged, and begged Mr. Bull to take the plantation into his own hands; however, Bull continued to fupply him with cafh, and he kept on making attempts. Alterations were made in the terms of fet-

tlement,

tlement, the reftrictions were removed, cattle and grog were allowed, Lord Strut was
oufted, and poffeffion held ; the fwamps
were drained ; rice and indigo were cultivated inftead of filk and wine ; and upon
the whole, confiderable improvements were
made, though at fuch a vaft expenfe, that
Mr. Bull never faw any adequate returns.

THE ill fuccefs of this adventure did not
deter him from another project.   He was
extremely fond of *Trout*,* and thought if
he could have them regularly catched and
brought to his table, he fhould exceed all
his neighbours in delicate living ; and now
and then be able to fend a mefs to his particular friends.   Lord Peter's family, too,
he thought, would be glad to buy them, as
they were very ufeful in the long lents,
and frequent meagre days obferved by
them.   There was a part of the foreft on
the north-eaft quarter, which was very con-
veniently fituated for this employment.   It
had been occupied by ALEXANDER SCOTUS,
a purblind

* Cod fifhery.

a purblind fellow, who had ſtraggled thither
no one could tell how ; and it was matter
of doubt whether he derived his right from
Bull, or Lewis ; for both of them laid
claim to the land, and their claims had not
been fairly decided in law. To make ſure
of the matter, Mr. Bull, by advice of his
wife, ſent a waggon to bring off the family
of Scotus, whom he diſtributed among the
other families of his tenants ; and in their
room ſent thither* a parcel of naked, half
ſtarved people, who could live no where
elſe, and ſupported them for ſeveral years
with proviſions, furniſhed them with ſkiffs,
lines, hooks and other implements to carry
on the fiſhery ; but every trout which they
catched, coſt him ten times as much as if
he had bought it in the common market ;
nor could he, after all, get half of what he
wanted for his own conſumption. His
trout fiſhery, and his mulberry plantation,
rendered him the laughing ſtock of his
neighbours, nor could he ever gain even
the intereſt of the money which he had laid

out

* 1749.

out upon them; while the forefters who had fettled at their own expenfe, grew rich and became refpectable. He had indeed the benefit of their trade, which kept his journeymen at work, and obliged him to enlarge their number; for the forefters had a refpect for their old mafter and landlord, and when they had any thing to fell, they always let him have the refufal of it, and bought all their goods of him.   But though he called himfelf their father, and his wife their mother, yet he began to abate of his parental affection for them ;   and rather looked on them with a jealous eye, as if they were aiming to deprive him of his claim, and fet up for independence.   Had he been contented with the profits of their trade, as was certainly his intereft, they might have remained his tenants to this day; but ambition, avarice, jealoufy and choler, inflamed by bad counfellors, have wrought fuch a feparation, that it is thought Mr. Bull will go mourning all the remainder of his days, and his grey hairs will be brought down with forrow to the grave.

Letter VIII.

Mr. BULL's *Quarrel and Law-Suit with* LEWIS *and Lord* STRUT.——*He gains Pof-feffion of the whole Foreft.*

DEAR SIR,

IN my former letters I have endeav-oured to trace the feveral fteps by which the foreft became cultivated and peopled. Mr. Bull had no lefs than fourteen tenants who held under him, and were fettled on lands which he claimed as his own, and which he had granted to them in feparate parcels. Their names, were as follows:

Alexander Scotus,	—————— Cafimir,
Robert Lumber,	William Broadbrim,
John Codline,	Cecilius Marygold,
Roger Carrier,	Walter Pipeweed,
	Humphry

Humphry Ploughſhare, Peter Pitch,
Peter Bullfrog,   Charles Indigo,
Julius Cæſar,   George Truſty.

It was obſerved that of all the adventurers, thoſe generally were the *leaſt thriving*,
who received *moſt aſſiſtance* from their old
maſter.   I cannot tell whether it was owing to their being employed in buſineſs to
which they had not ſerved a regular ap-
prenticeſhip, or to a natural indolence, and
a diſpoſition to continue hangers-on where
they had got a good hold ; for it muſt be
noted, that Mr. Bull was very generous to
ſome perſons, and on ſome occaſions where
it ſuited his fancy; and this diſpoſition in
him was ſo prevalent, that they who ken-
ned him, and would humour his whims,
could work him out of any thing which
they had a mind to.

On the other hand, thoſe adventurers
who came into the foreſt on their own account, and had no aſſiſtance at all from
their old maſter, nor any thing to help
themſelves

themfelves with, but their four limbs and five fenfes, proved to be the moft induftrious and thriving, and after a while told up a good eftate. They all feemed to have an affection for Mr. Bull, and it was generally believed to be fincere. His houfe was ufually fpoken of by them as their *home*. His ware-houfe was the centre of their traffic; and he had the addrefs to engrofs the profits of their labour, and draw their earnings into his own fob. To fome of them he would now and then make a prefent, to others he would lend a pack of his hounds, when he was out of the humour of hunting; but they were generally ufelefs to them for the purpofe of fcouring the woods; thofe who could afford it, kept dogs of their own, who were better trained to the game, and could better fcent the foreft, being native curs, and not fo fpruce and delicate a breed as Bull's grey-hounds.

It has been before obferved, that each end of the foreft was occupied by Bull's rivals. His old neighbour Lewis had got the

the north end, and Lord Strut the fouth. Bull's tenants had feated themfelves chiefly on or near the fhore of the lake, and had not extended very far back, becaufe of the beafts of prey; but Lewis, like a cunning old fox, had formed a fcheme to get footing in the interior parts of the country, and prevent thefe planters from penetrating beyond the limits which he intended to affign them. His emiffaries had been fent flily into the diftant parts of the foreft, under pretence of taming thefe beafts of prey; but in fact they had halved the matter with them, and had themfelves become as favage as the beafts had become tame. They would run, leap and climb with them, and crawl into their dens, imparting to them a lick of *molaffes* out of their calabáfh, and teaching them to fcratch with their paws the fign of a crofs. They had built feveral hunting lodges on the moft convenient paffes of the brooks and ponds, and though thus fcattered in the wood, they were all united under one overfeer, called ONONTIO, who

lived

lived in the manfion-houfe of St. Lewis's Hall.

It was matter of wonder among Bull's tenants, for fome time, what could be the reafon that the wild beafts had grown more furly and fnappifh of late than formerly; but after a while, fome hunters made a difcovery of the new lodges, which the emiffaries of Onontio had erected, and the defign of them being apparent, a general alarm was raifed in the plantations. On the firft news, Walter Pipeweed fent his grandfon *George*, a fmart, active, lively youth, acrofs the hills, with his compliments to the intruders, defiring them to move off, and threatening them with a writ, in cafe of non-compliance.* This modeft warning being ineffectual, it was thought that if an *Union* could be formed among the tenants, they might make a ftand againft thefe encroachments. A meeting was held at *Orange Hall*,† but no efficient plan could be hit on, without a previous application to

H   their

* 1753.   † Albany, 1754.

their landlord, who hearing of this meeting, conceived a jealoufy with regard to this *union* which feemed to be their object, and thought it was better to retain the management of the matter in his own hands, and keep them divided among themfelves, but united in their dependence on him. He therefore fent them word that " he had a very great affection for them, and would take care of *their* intereft, which was alfo *his own ;* that he would not fuffer Lewis to fet his half tamed wild beafts upon them, nor eject them from their poffeffions, but that he would immediately take advice of his council, learned in the law, conjuring them by the affection which they profeffed to bear towards him, to be aiding and affifting in all ways in their power, towards bringing the controverfy to an iffue.

At this time, the fteward, to whom Mr. Bull entrufted the care of his bufinefs, was not a perfon of that difcernment and expedition which the exigency of affairs required. He had committed divers blunders in

his

his accounts, and it was fufpected that he was a defaulter in more refpects than one. It cannot, therefore, be expected, that in conducting a controverfy of this magnitude, he fhould exactly hit on the right methods, nor employ the beft council which could be had. The firft ftep taken was to fend *Broadoak** the bailiff, with a writ of intrufion, which he was ordered to ferve *volens nolens*, upon one of the meffuages or hunting-feats of Lewis. This bailiff, proceeding rafhly and againft the beft advice into the foreft, not a ftep of which he was acquainted with, found his progrefs impeded in a way wholly unexpected. For Onontio had taken care to place a number of his half tamed wild-cats and wolverenes on the boughs of trees, which hung over the path, and as foon as the bailiff came within reach, having firft wetted their tails with their own urine, they whifked it into his eyes till they blinded him. This manoeuvre put a ftop to the procefs for that time.

H 2   SEVERAL

* Braddock, 1755.

SEVERAL other attempts of the like kind were made without fuccefs, and *Lewis* at one time had almoft got poffeffion of *Orange Hall.** Not only the forefters themfelves, but even Bull's own domeftics, complained bitterly of thefe ineffectual meafures, and their clamors at laft prevailed to make him difcharge his old fteward, and put another into his place. The new officer† foon changed the face of affairs ; he employed no attorneys, nor bailiffs, but thofe of tried and approved abilities, men of enterprife and refolution, by whom the fuit was profecuted in good earneft. In every action Bull recovered judgment, and got poffeffion. When Lord Strut came in to the aid of Lewis, Bull caft him alfo, and took away his manor of Auguftine, which, with the whole tract of land, where Onontio prefided, was annexed to his eftate. The agents who had been employed in this arduous fervice, were not only well paid for doing their duty, but, with the fteward who employed them, were honoured according to the ancient

* 1757.   † Pitt's adminiftration.

cient but whimfical cuftom of Bull's family, by having their effigies pourtrayed on fign-boards, pocket handkerchiefs, fnuff-boxes, and punch-bowls; fo that while the fit lafted, you could not walk the ftreets, nor blow your nofe, nor take a pinch of fnuff, nor a draught of punch, but you were obliged to *falute* them.

WHENEVER Bull's fteward called upon the forefters for their quotas of aid towards carrying on this heavy law-fuit, they always readily afforded it; and fome of them were really almoft exhaufted by the efforts which they made, to do *more* than their fhare. The fteward was fo fenfible of their merit, that on due confultation with Mr. Bull's wife, and her taking him in the right mood, he was prevailed upon to reimburfe the extra expenfe to them, and mutual complacency reigned between the landlord and tenants all the time this fteward remained in office. But thefe times were too good to laft long; there were fome who envied the fteward his reputation, and raifed ftories

to

to his difadvantage, which highly affronted him.   At this time Mr. Bull was fo much off his guard, as to give heed to thefe reports, and take a rafh ftep in a hurry, which he had occafion to repent of at his leifure.   He accepted the refignation of this trufty fervant, and put one of his* fifter Peg's caft off footmen into his place ; whereby he laid a foundation for his own difgrace, and the difmemberment of his eftate, of which I fhall give you a particular account hereafter.   ADIEU.

* Bute's adminiftration, 1761.

Letter IX.

Mr. BULL *gets into Debt, and by the Advice of his new Wife and her gambling Companions, begins a Quarrel with his Tenants.*

DEAR SIR,

To trace with precision all the causes, great and small, which operated to the dismemberment of John Bull's estate, would be no easy task ; some of them perhaps, were *secret,* but of such as were open to observation, we shall endeavour to sketch out the principal.

It is well known that he was of a choleric habit, and that those who were acquainted with his humor and passions, could manage and impose upon him at their pleasure. Had he been let alone to

pursue

purſue his own buſineſs *himſelf*, his plain,
natural good ſenſe, and generoſity of mind,
would have kept him clear of many difficulties ; but he had his adviſers, his hangers-on, his levee-hunters, his toad-eaters,
and ſycophants, forever about him, who,
like a parcel of blood-ſuckers, could never
have enough to glut their voracity.

WHEN the foreſt was firſt occupied by
the tenants, Bull had a wife who minded
her own domeſtic buſineſs, and did not
concern herſelf with his landed intereſt.
The leaſes and grants were made out in
his name, and he was ſuppoſed to be the
owner or proprietor ; but the lady whom
he had married after his ſecond ſickneſs,
was very aſſuming, and inſiſted on having
her hand in the management of *all* his
affairs.   She viſited the compting-houſe,
and made the clerks ſhew her their books ;
ſhe overhauled the ſteward's accounts, and
inſpected his correſpondence ; ſhe not only
looked after the rents and incomes of the
foreſt, but even intruded into the houſehold
concerns

concerns of the tenants, and affected to call herfelf *their mother*, becaufe fhe had taken fome care of one or two of them in their firft fetting out, although moft of them fcarcely ever had feen her face, or had any acquaintance with her, but by hearfay.

It muft be obferved, alfo, that this wo-man had engaged Mr. Bull in fome expen-five law-fuits and fpeculations, which had got him deeply into *debt*, and he was obli-ged to hire money of ufurers to carry her fchemes into execution. Had fhe, at the fame time, introduced that frugality and economy into the family, which her duty ought to have prompted her to, this debt might have been kept down ; but the fwarm of harpies which were continually about her, and the courfe of gambling which was carried on under her conni-vance and direction, fwallowed up all the profits of the trade, and incomes of the land ; while the luxury and diffipation of the family *increafed*, in proportion as the

means

means of difcharging the debt *de*creafed.
In fhort, Mr. Bull was reduced to that
humiliating condition, which, by whatever
fafhionable name it may now go, was
formerly called *petticoat government*.

DURING the law-fuit with Lewis and
Lord Strut,* concerning the foreft, there
had been a great intercourfe with the tenants. Many of Bull's fervants and retainers, who were employed as bailiffs and attornies, and their deputies, had been very
converfant with them, and were entertained
at their houfes, where they always found
wholefome victuals, jolly fire fides, and
warm beds. They took much notice of
every thing that paffed, afked many quef-
tions, and made many remarks on the goodnefs of the land, the pleafant fituation of
the houfes, the clean and thriving condition
of the children, who were always ready to
wait on them, to clean their boots, hold
their ftirrups, open and fhut the gates for
them, and the like little neceffary fervices,

as

* War of 1756.

as well bred children in the country are wont. The remarks which thefe perfons made, when they got home, favored rather of envy, than of gratitude or affection. Some of them would fay : " Thofe fellows live too well in the foreft ; they thrive too faft ; the place is too good for them ; they ought to know who is their mafter ; they can afford to pay more rent ; they ought to pay for the help they have had ; if it had not been for Mafter Bull, and the affift-ance which he has lent them, they would have been turned out of doors ; and now they are to reap the benefit of his exertions, while he, poor man, is to pay the coft."

THERE were not wanting fome, in the families of the Forefters themfelves, who had the meannefs to crouch to thefe fel-lows, and fupplicate their favour and inte-reft with Mr. Bull, to recommend them to fome pofts of profit, as under-ftewards, col-lectors of rent, clerks of receipts, and the like petty offices. Thefe beggarly curs would repeat the fame language, and hold
correfpondence

correfpondence with the bailiffs, attornies, &c. after they had got home. Whenever any trifling quarrel happened in the families of the tenants, they would magnify it, and fill their letters with complaints of the licentioufnefs of the people, and plead for a tighter hand to be held over them.

Such fpeeches as thefe were frequently made, and fuch letters read, in the hearing of Mr. Bull's wife and fteward. Their language grew by degrees to be the current language of the family, and Bull himfelf liftened to it. His choler rofe upon the occafion, and when his hangers-on obferved it, they plied him with ftronger dofes, till his jealoufy and hatred were excited, and a complete revolution in his temper, with regard to his tenants, took place, agreeably to the moft fanguine and malevolent wifhes of his and their enemies.

THE firft effect of this change was, that his clerks were ordered to charge not only the prices of the goods, which the tenants

fhould

should purchase, but to make them pay for the *paper** on which their bills of parcels and notes of hand were written, and that at a very exorbitant rate. This was so intolerable an abuse, and withal so mean, pitiful and beggarly an expedient to pick their pockets, that they held a meeting among themselves, and resolved not to buy any more of his goods, as long as this imposition lasted ; and by way of contempt, they hanged and burned the effigies of the steward, and other persons who were suspected of having advised to these new measures.

THE resentment shewn by the tenants on this occasion was quite unexpected. The secret favourers, and real authors of the mischief, began to be afraid that they had gone too far for the first attempt. Bull's journeymen were in an uproar about it, lest, by the failure of his trade, they should be out of bread ; and to shorten the story, he was obliged to give up the point of making them pay for the paper ; though

Madam

* Stamp act, 1765.

Madam had the fingular modefty to make a declaration, that it was a mere matter of *expediency*, and that fhe had power and right "to bind them in all cafes whatfoever," notwithftanding Mr. Bull's *moft gracious* conceffion at that time.[*]

THIS was confidered by the tenants as a moft impudent and barefaced affumption ; for whatever rights Mr. Bull might pretend to have as their old mafter and landlord, yet they never had any idea of a *miftrefs* over them ; and though they very complaifantly returned him their thanks for his prefent goodnefs, yet as they fufpected that there was more mifchief hatching, they began to inquire more narrowly than ever into his right and title to the land on which they lived. They looked over old parchments and memorandums, confulted council learned in the law, and after due deliberation, they were fully convinced, that *their own* title was at leaft as good as *his*, and that they had a right to refufe him any

rent

[*] Repeal of the ftamp act, and declaratory act, 1766.

rent or acknowledgment, if it were prudent
for them to exercise it.

MR. Bull's jealousy was now increased
with regard to their intentions, and his
scribbling retainers frequently accused them
of ingratitude and disobedience, and a long
premeditated design to set up for *independence* ; a thing which they had not yet
thought of, and probably never would, if
this abusive treatment had not put it into
their heads.

BUT though by those means they were
led into an inquiry, and a train of thinking,
which were quite new to them ; yet as old
habits are not easily broken, and their affection for their master was very strong, they
endeavoured, with a candour which did them
honour, to transfer the blame from him to
his wife and steward, to whose machina-
tions they knew he was a dupe. These bad
counsellors soon renewed their attempts in
another shape, by raising the rent, and putting an advanced price upon the goods ; and
by

by means of additional clerks, packers, porters, watchmen, draymen, &c. who were
continually in waiting, and to all of whom
fees were to be paid, the trade laboured
under great embarraffments, and fome of
the forefters were quite difcouraged, others
were vexed and impatient, while fome of
the better tempered of them, endeavoured
to perfuade the reft to keep up the commu-
nication as long as they could.   They were
loth to quarrel with their old mafter, and
yet could not pocket the affronts and abufes
to which they were daily expofed.

DURING this fullen interval, many letters
paffed, many books and precedents were
examined, and much ink was fhed, in a
controverfy, which, however incapable of
a *decifion* in this way, might have been *com-
promifed*, if Mr. Bull's firft thoughts had
been as good as his fecond ; but he was fo
completely under management, as not to
fee his true intereft.   It was a common
faying among his neighbours, " John Bull's
wit comes afterward ;" and in fact it did

not

not come, in this cafe, till too late, for when a caufe once gets into the law, there are fo many quirks, evafions, demurs, and procraftinations, that it is impoffible to make a retreat, till one or both of the parties have feverely fmarted for their temerity.

I

Letter X.

Mr. BULL attempts a new Mode of Traffic which difgufts his Tenants.——They refuse to receive his Prefents.——His fingular Refentment againft JOHN CODLINE, and the Effects which it produced.

DEAR SIR,

I SUPPOSE you are by this time impatient for the ftory of the law-fuit; how it began, and how it was carried on and ended. I will give it to you as briefly as fo long and intricate a matter will bear to be told; and I am apprehenfive you will think that Mr. Bull was fo ill a politician, or fo badly advifed, as actually to pick a quarrel with his beft cuftomers. But facts will fpeak for themfelves. Know then, that by the advice of his dear wife, and

her

her gambling junto, Mr. Bull was prevailed upon to fend a dozen pounds of tea to each of his tenants, *as a prefent*, in token of his extreme good will to them, and becaufe he knew that they loved it; and at the fame time to order his clerks to charge *three pence* for the paper and pack-thread in which each pound of this exhilerating weed was wrapped. This trifling fum he expected would be paid on demand, in acknowledgment of their good will to him as their kind and generous landlord, who had protected and defended them againft all oppofers, and would ftill continue to protect and defend them as his beloved children, and obedient humble fervants.

The knowledge of his intention happened to come to them fooner than the prefent, and they began to argue thus among themfelves—"Ha! how comes this? What is freer than a gift? If Mr. Bull really intends the tea as a prefent, why does he exact three pence? Had he offered it to us as an article of merchandife,

as ufual, we might have taken it if we had
liked the price, or left it if we had not;
but this is a new way of trading to which
we have not been accuftomed. There is a
defign in this. If we receive this prefent
and pay the trifling acknowledgment of
three pence, by and by we fhall have a prefent with fix pence annexed, and another
with a fhilling, and fo on. If we once
eftablifh a precedent, there is no knowing
where to ftop, and by thefe prefents we
may be gulled out of all our loofe corns,
and afterwards our real eftates may be de-
manded! No, it is better to prevent an
evil than to cure it. We will have none of
your prefents, Mr. Bull, if this is to be the
confequence. We have paid our debts
well—you have had the *exclufive* benefit of
our trade, and have become rich by it, and
now in your old age you are grown trick-
ifh. It is time for us to be on our guard
and keep a fharp look out; for if a man
does not take care of himfelf, who can he
expect will take care of him?" Fortified
with thefe arguments, they waited for the
approach

approach of the meffengers, who were on the road with the prefents.

ONE of them came to Charles Indigo's houfe, and with Mr. Bull's compliments begged his acceptance of a package of tea. "Throw it into that cellar, faid Charles, and let it lie there till I have confidered of the matter."

ANOTHER came to William Broadbrim —but as the way to William's manfion was through a long, crooked, miry lane, he had ordered the porter to ftop him, and give him liberty to return without delivering his meffage.

PETER BULLFROG did the fame; but fome part of the tea being fmuggled into the houfe, as foon as Peter knew it, he threw it into the gutter.

JOHN CODLINE had the greateft difficulty about Mr. Bull's prefent. He would gladly have fent back the meffenger, but unluckily

luckily for him, the gate which led to his houfe was held faft by Bull's *Under Steward*, who conftantly watched and attended there, to obferve who went in and out, which fervice he was more particularly fond of, becaufe he expected a douceur for opening and fhutting the gate. Having admitted the meffenger and received his *penny*, he ftiflly refufed to let him out again without having delivered the prefent. The *fee* was tendered, but this could not prevail; the family were uneafy, they were loth to affront Mr. Bull, and yet determined not to receive his prefent. They could not account for the conduct of the under fteward on any other principle than this, that he expected to get a fhare of the *three pence*, and of all other profits arifing from future prefents; and was afraid he fhould lofe it if he let the meffenger return. The family was called together in the chapel, where they held a long confultation, fent feveral meffages to the under fteward, who held faft the gate, and finally refufed to open it. They were driven at length to an extremity, and

threw

threw the tea into the vault, where it perifhed, at the fame time protefting that the
whole blame ought to be charged on the
under fteward, as they had no intention of
injuring Mr. Bull if they could have avoid-
ed it.

As foon as this was known in Mr. Bull's
family, his wife fell into a violent hyfteric
fit, and in her raving phrenzy denounced
all the vengeance which it was in her power to execute, on thefe refractory, ungrateful tenants, who would not accept a prefent when it was fo freely offered to them.
But when fhe came a little to herfelf, fhe
was perfuaded by her gambling companions
not to attempt any thing againft the whole
body of the tenants, left they fhould be
driven by neceffity to form an union a-
mong themfelves, which might defeat the
plan; fhe therefore *propofed* to Mr. Bull to
fingle out *one* of the moft refractory of
them, and fhew his refentment in a particular manner to *him*, hoping that the others
would be intimidated and let him fuffer
alone,

alone, and be glad to get off fo well themfelves.   The perfon fingled out for the object of refentment was John Codline, and
the mode of refentment, was as ridiculous
as it was malicious, for it was nothing
more nor lefs than to fend a bailiff, with a
pack of blood-hounds, to ftand before the
great gate that led to the *front* of his houfe.*
This, it was thought, would ftrengthen the
authority of the under fteward who had the
key of the gate, and would reduce the family to this dilemma, either to receive no
company and carry on no bufinefs, or elfe to
fubmit to Mr. Bull's new mode of trading.

THE reafon affigned for this particular
mode of revenge was, that Mr. Bull, as
lord of the manor, claimed a kind of fove-
reign right to the high way.   He had for
a long time exacted an acknowledgment
from all paffengers ; whenever they happened to meet any of his horfes or carriages
on the road, whether he was there himfelf
or not, they were obliged to *doufe* the hat,

or

* Bofton Port Act, 1774.

or they might be sure of receiving a stroke of the whip, if not of being run down by his servants, who had special orders not to let any omission of this nature pass unpunished.

In consequence of this manœuvre on the part of Mr. Bull, every person who had any business to do with John Codline was stopped in the road, and ordered to go back, or pass by, like the Priest and Levite, on the other side. However, those who had a mind to see him, found means to climb over the fence, or to go up a narrow lane, which, by the help of a stile and a foot path, led them to Codline's back door.

This species of punishment exposed Mr. Bull to the ridicule of all his neighbours. It also proved quite ineffectual to the purpose for which he designed it. Instead of hindering company from coming to Codline's house, it brought more; and he received many letters from those who could not come in person. But, what was of

more

more fervice to him than letters or vifits was this, that many who were indebted to him came and made payment, and thofe who had at various times received favours from him when they were in diftrefs, fent him prefents, and encouraged him to keep up a good heart, promifing to ftand by him to the laft extremity, if he fhould be reduced to it.

IT has been obferved, that one advantage which Mrs. Bull expected would arife from this fpecimen of her *refined* policy was, that it would difunite the tenants, and frighten fome or perhaps all the others into a compliance with the new mode of traffic. This expectation was grounded on one of the fables of Efop, which relates, that a fox who had been caught in a trap, and difengaged himfelf by the lofs of his tail, whenever he appeared among the foxes, was the object of their ridicule; upon which, he endeavoured to perfuade them that he had been travelling to learn fafhions, and that the neweft fafhion was for foxes to cut off

their

their tails as a ufelefs and burdenfome appendage, and boafted how much more light and nimble he had become fince he had parted with that incumbrance; to which an old fox replied, that if he would do juftice to his argument, he ought to produce the *fhears* with which he had cut off his tail, for the conviction of his brethren.

THIS fable, and the moral couched under it, raifed a great deal of vain expectation and triumph in the family of Mr. Bull; but the forefters had another of their own making, which was a match for it. A man meeting a ferpent in the field, ftruck at him with a ftick, and there being but one in his view he thought to kill him immediately; but the fnake fet up fuch a hifs as brought a dozen more out of their holes, who attacked the proud murderer in front, rear, and flank, and obliged him to take to his heels for fafety. This fable was fo much admired among the forefters at that time, that they had an engraving made on all their meffage cards, of a wounded ferpent, with this motto, *Join or die.* ADIEU.

Letter XI.

The Quarrel begins in earneſt and is carried into the Law.——Conduct of the Managers on both Sides.——The firſt Verdict in favour of the Foreſters given at Saratoga Hall.

DEAR SIR,

THE inſult which the foreſters ſuppoſed to be put on them by the obſtruction, of the road, as mentioned in my laſt, cauſed a ſerious alarm, and induced them to call a meeting of the heads of the ſeveral families to conſult for their own ſafety. The reſult of this meeting was to endeavour, by all peaceable means in their power, to effect an accommodation; but if that ſhould fail, to prepare, in the beſt manner they could, to aſſert and maintain their rights, poſſeſſions and properties.

IN.

IN profecution of the former part of their plan, they wrote letters to Mr. Bull, and to feveral members of his family; and with refpect to the latter part, they came to a refolution to buy nothing more of him till he fhould change his mode of conduct, and treat them as he had formerly done.

IN the letters which they wrote on this occafion, though they profeffed a great deal of refpect and affection for the old gentleman himfelf; they *omitted* to fend their compliments to his wife. This was more than Madam could bear. She therefore, after confulting with her gambling companions, determined upon the two following points; firft, that no anfwer at all fhould be given to the letter; and fecondly, that an action at law fhould be entered, and the tenants ejected from their poffeffions. She would not however have come to this latter determination, if fhe had not been affured by perfons who pretended thoroughly to underftand their family fecrets, that the forefters *would not dare to defend*

defend their title in law; but on the firft appearance of a legal procefs, would fubmit to any terms of accommodation which her ladyfhip might think proper to impofe. Full of this idea, fhe roundly fwore that fhe would fee them *proftrate at her feet*, before fhe would make up the matter with them on any terms whatever.

INFLUENCED by her paffions, Mr. Bull's choler rofe to the higheft pitch. As lord of the manor, he placed bailiffs and bloodhounds in the high way, and denied all paffage to any perfons without his licenfe. He then called upon all the counfellors and attornies to whom he had given a retaining fee, and who were very numerous, to exert all their learning and eloquence in maintaining his caufe, promifing them not only a regular payment of their fees, but a generous allowance for difburfements and incidental charges, to be paid at fight by a draught on his banker; and when the caufe fhould be gained, that each one

fhould

should be entitled to a plantation in the
forest.

THESE sagacious gentlemen, (many of
whom were of Madam's own junto) finding that they had a fat client, contrived to
husband the job, and spin out the cause
secundum artem. They were old profi-
cients in the science, and knew very well
how to take double receipts of their sta-
tioners, bailiffs, messengers, and other retainers, *i. e.* one receipt for the exact sum
paid, and another for *double* the same sum;
these latter were always produced as vouch-
ers in the settlement of accounts, and in
the glorious uncertainty of the law were
admitted under the name of *duplicates.* It
would divert you to see the numberless
items which they crowded into their bills
of cost, and the various pleas and pretences which were formed for demurring
and continuing the cause from one session
to another; while they were feeding their
client with the hope that in every *next*
session it would be decided.

On

ON the other hand, the foresters finding that Mr. Bull had retained so many learned counsellors, serjeants and barristers in his service, and that he had by far the longest purse, were obliged to use the greatest economy in conducting their defence. On looking round to see who was the most prudent, the most deliberate, and the most determined among them, and to whom they might with safety commit their cause, they unanimously pitched upon *Walter Pipeweed's* grandson *George*; who, being elected their chief attorney, modestly accepted the office on this generous condition, that they should not insist on his receiving any fee or reward, because he conceived that in serving them he was doing no more than his duty. This instance of magnanimity was interpreted by them as a sure omen of success.

GEORGE was a man of good understanding and true spunk ; he had made considerable progress in the study of the law for his own amusement, and had practised at

the

the bar in the defence of his own family claims againſt the encroachments of Lewis. His abilities were of ſuch a nature as to riſe and ſhine with the opportunities which called them into action. This was alſo the caſe with divers other perſons in the families of the foreſters; who would, perhaps, never have thought of engaging in the ſtudy of the law, had not this controverſy been agitated; but would have remained in the ſtate which is thus elegantly deſcribed by the poet.

> " Full many a gem of pureſt ray ſerene,
>   The dark unfathom'd caves of ocean bear;
> Full many a flower is born to bluſh unſeen,
>   And waſte its ſweetneſs on the defart air."

THIS circumſtance was predicted in the hearing of Mr. Bull's wife, by a very learned and honeſt gentleman, who would have diſſuaded her from giving her huſband ſuch bad advice as to plunge himſelf into that deep ditch, the law, out of which there is no coming till the laſt farthing be paid.

" If

" If there are any feeds of genius," faid
this faithful advifer, " they are drawn into
action by public ferments and troubles ; but
might have remained in time of tranquillity
forever ufelefs and unknown, perhaps at
the plough, under a fhed, or among the
loweft clafs of mechanics."*   This fage
hint was totally difregarded, becaufe, as I
before obferved, too much confidence was
placed in a fet of advifers, who pretended
to know all the family fecrets of the forefters.   But the prediction was fully verified
when this law-fuit brought to the bar one
from his farm, and another from his mer-
chandize, one from his fhed, and another
from his fhop,† till in fact they became a
                                    match,

* Vide Debates in Parliament, March 16, 1775.

 . † This circumftance gave occafion to the following
bagatelle, written, as is fuppofed, by fome difaffected
or perhaps difappointed wag, in one of the families,

See folly on a lofty feat,
And humble wifdom at her feet !
On horfeback fee the beggar ride,
With princes walking by his fide.

Pale

match, in point of numbers at leaft, for the whole hoft of Mr. Bull's attornies.

THE firft action was brought againft John Codline, who was deemed the moft furly and refractory of the whole number. It was thought if he could be caft, the others would of courfe fubmit.   In this way of proceeding, Mr. Bull acted like that fpecies of dog which bears his name, and which is known to attack his enemy by the head.

THE caufe was learnedly argued at the Court of *Bunker hall*, and the arguments in favour of the forefters made a very unexpected

> Pale Crifpin has his laft foregone,
> To ferve himfelf and fave his town
> And Snip the taylor's fhears are loft,
> Becaufe he's got a higher poft.
>
> So have I feen the kitchen pot,
> When fet on coals profufely hot,
> Throw up its fediment to fcum,
> While bubbles dance amidft the foam.

K 2

expected and very deep impreffion on the managers for Mr. Bull. They found it a much more ferious affair than they had imagined, and thought it beft to ftop fhort and have the cafe *hung up*, that they might confult their books over again, and prepare themfelves by better authorities and allegations at the next hearing. After a long time they contrived to *fhift their ground*,* and let John alone. They advifed Mr. Bull to fend for fome lawyers out of Germany, who had been more ufed to this kind of pleading, and to lay an attachment on the eftate of Peter Bullfrog, and the farm called Cæfarea; where they expected to gain fome greater advantage, partly becaufe the tenancy was different, being founded on courtefy and not on leafe, and partly becaufe of the diffentions which they heard were fubfifting in thefe families. In this interval alfo Madam Bull's refentment was raifed fo high, that fhe fwore point blank that not one of thefe refractory fcoundrels fhould enter her hufband's doors, nor have

* March, 1776.

have the leaft connexion with him, but that fhe would drive them off from the land, and re-people the foreft with another fet of men.

WHEN they had heard of this refolution, the heads of all the families in one of their confultations, came to a determination to publifh an advertifement, fetting forth the various abufes and grievances which they had fuffered from Mr. Bull, his wife, and her junto; and declaring that they looked upon the country as *their own*, and themfelves free from any obligations to him, and at liberty to look out for other markets, and invite other merchants to form connexions with them. This tranfaction was fo important an era in the controverfy, that the *fourth of July*, the day on which the advertifement was dated, has ever fince been celebrated as a day of feftivity. The morning of that anniverfary is ufhered in with a firing of guns and fluttering of pigeons. At noon you may hear fome young lad fpouting a declamation in favour of free trade;

trade; which is generally followed by a bowl of punch and a rump of beef, and the day is concluded with a fong and a dance.

In the progrefs of the action, feveral points of law were argued at different times with much fkill and learning. On one of thefe occafions George was reduced to a dilemma, and his opponents thought him abfolutely filenced; but fuddenly recollecting himfelf, he rofe fuperior to them,* and compelled them again to move for a continuance. Thus the caufe was kept fufpended till the *third year* was almoft clofed. At length a vaunting braggadocio of a barrifter on Mr. Bull's fide, who thought to carry all before him, was fo completely anfwered and confuted in an obftinate argument, that a verdict was given at *Saratoga hall* in favour of thofe plantations, which had been fued for in the northern part of the manor. This verdict relieved the forefters in fome degree, and it

was

* Trenton, 1776.

was hoped would prove a good precedent for the decifion of the other fuits which were meditating againft their brethren in the fouthern part.

THE unfortunate barrifter was feverely reflected on by Mr. Bull's wife, for not doing his duty; and he was obliged to juftify himfelf by producing his inftructions, and by telling a number of ferious truths refpecting the foreft and the forefters, which Mrs. Bull had often heard before but would not believe. The relation of thefe truths was fo very offenfive that fhe influenced her hufband never more to employ him; and as he could get no other bufinefs in the law, he afterward employed himfelf in writing plays and romances, in which he was more fuccefsful.

Letter XII.

The Foreſters apply for Help to Mr. Lewis
—are firſt treated with Evaſion—after-
ward obtain their Requeſt—Alarm in Mr.
Bull's *Family—His Conference with his*
Wife—Her Manœuvres upon the Occaſion
—Diſappointed by the Inflexibility of the
Foreſters.

DEAR SIR,

You may well ſuppoſe that
a three years law-ſuit was a very expenſive
undertaking on both ſides; and you will
wonder how the foreſters, circumſtanced
as they were, could ſtruggle with ſuch an
antagoniſt; eſpecially when the high way
was ſo obſtructed that they could not carry their proviſions to market to procure them
caſh.   The truth is, that though they were
ſerved

served *gratis* by their prime counsellor, yet they were obliged to give promissory notes to the attornies, scriveners, bailiffs, and messengers, whom they employed under him; but as the prospect of payment was distant, the notes passed at a discount, and the only remedy in their power was to issue *more*, which instead of lessening increased the difficulty.

THEY had early foreseen this difficulty; and applied privately to Mr. Lewis, Mr. Frog, and Lord Strut, to borrow money on interest. These old curmudgeons, though each of them looked with an envious eye on Mr. Bull, and secretly wished he might lose the cause, yet were induced by various considerations to evade the question proposed to them by the foresters. " We must, said they, keep up appearances with our old neighbour ; we have accounts open with him, as well as claims upon some portions of land, to which our title is no better than his ; we may draw ourselves into a scrape, and set our own tenants a bad example,

example, for who knows but the fame arguments may avail with them to refufe
their rents to us? Befides, how do we
know whether thefe fellows will ever be
able to pay? They offer to mortgage the
manor to us, but the title is yet in difpute,
and how do we know whether it be their's
or Mr. Bull's?" Thefe were the fecret
reafons which induced them to evade a direct anfwer to the meffengers; and, like true
courtiers,

"To fqueeze their hands, and beg them come to-
    morrow."

BUT as foon as the verdict was given at
Saratoga hall, they began to change their
mind, and wifhed not only to make them
debtors, but even to enter into contracts to
a large amount.

MR. Lewis was the firft to make advan-
ces, and meeting the meffengers one day on
'change, he accofted them thus: " Your
fervant, gentlemen—I congratulate you on
your fuccefs; you are welcome to my houfe,
                                        and

and ware-houfe, and table. I will lend you
a few livres to help you to finiſh the controverſy; and if Mr. Frog will advance a
few ſtivers, I will give him my bond for ſe-
curity. Beſides, I will conſent that my own
counſellors, barriſters, and attornies, whom
I have retained, ſhall aſſiſt you at the next
ſeſſion, and I will ſee if I cannot open the
high way, that you may bring your produce to market. When you ſee Lord
Strut, give my compliments to him, and
tell him what I have promiſed, and I dare
ſay he will, out of friendſhip to *me*, and for
the ſake of our old *family compact*, give you
ſome aſſiſtance; for look ye, gentlemen, I
will be honeſt with you, I mean to promote
my own intereſt by ſerving you, and I am
ſure he has the ſame meaning.

THIS change in the ſentiments and language of Mr. Lewis, was immediately made
known to Mr. Bull, by means of ſome running footmen, who frequently carried news
from one houfe to the other. Conſternation
ſeized the whole family, and Mrs. Bull herſelf

felf began to think it a very ferious matter, and that it was neceffary to do fomething immediately to prevent worfe confequences. She therefore held a *curtain* conference with Mr. Bull on the fubject, thus—

Mrs. B. Well, my dear, what do you think of the conduct of your neighbour Lewis ?

Mr. B. Why I think he is a deceitful dog, and means to ruin me. If thefe fellows get him for their friend, he will draw in Lord Strut and Nic Frog, and I fhall have them all to contend with at once ; and therefore I think we had better compromife the matter with the tenants, and let them take the land, if they will, and go to the D-v-l ; why fhould I keep on throwing away good money after bad ; I am over head and ears in debt now, and I wifh to flop where I am, without getting any deeper into the law.

Mrs. B. I agree with you, my dear, that he is a deceitful dog, and I wifh the

tenants

tenants could know his true character : if they did, I am perfuaded they would not put any confidence in him. There is a number of very fenfible perfons among them, and by the difcourfe which I have had with fome who know their fecrets, I believe that means might yet be found to *divide* them, and to *detach* them from the interest of Lewis ; and if you will let me manage the matter, I have no doubt that I fhall be able to accomplifh it.

Poor John fetched a deep figh, and faid *inwardly*——Ah, I have let you manage my matters fo long, that you have almoft brought me to ruin ! Then raifing his voice and wiping his eyes, he replied, Well, my dear, I have told you *my* mind plainly, but if you think you can do any thing to fave me, pray be fpeedy ; I would gladly keep the tenants attached to me for the benefit of their trade, which is a matter of more confequence than their rent, and if I fhould finally lofe the land, I wifh to be again connected with them in bufinefs.

Mrs.

Mrs. B. Never fear, I do not doubt but we shall find means to keep the land and have the trade too. I know how to sweeten them and bring them to good humour again.

As soon as this conference was ended, she wrote a billet in a very complaisant style, but in a hand scarcely legible,* and was in such a hurry to send it, that she could not wait for one of the clerks to copy it, presenting Mr. and Mrs. Bull's compliments to the gentlemen tenants, informing them that it was not intended to trouble them any farther for the payment of paper and pack-thread, which had been the occasion of the controversy; but to settle all matters by a reference, and that suitable persons should soon be deputed to confer with them, or any of them on the premises. This billet was hurried away by an express, and actually arrived before the foresters had heard of Mr. Lewis's intended kindness to them. But they received it with contempt,

* 1778.

tempt, and gave no other anfwer to it than this, "Let Mr. Bull withdraw his action and clear the road, and we will talk with *him* ; but as to *his wife*, we will have nothing to do with *her*."

AFTER they had given this anfwer, word was brought them of the good will of Mr. Lewis, which was received with the greateft joy imaginable. He was accounted the fineft gentleman in the whole country, and all the ftories which they had heard of him, through the medium of Bull's family, were fet down as lies. He was regarded as the protector of the injured, the helper of the diftreffed, and the friend of the rights of mankind.

❧ WHILE the praifes of Lewis were thus echoed from houfe to houfe, the deputies of Madam Bull arrived. They were inftructed by her ladyfhip to enter into free converfation with the forefters, or any of them, publickly or privately ; to tell them that they were greatly deceived if they took

Mr.

Mr. Lewis for their friend ; that he was an arch, fly, deceitful fellow, and that no truft ought to be put in him ; that Mr. and Mrs. Bull were very amicably difpofed toward them, and willing to forget and forgive all that was paft, to renew the former intercourfe, to take off all the charges and burdens which had been complained of ; to help them to pay the debt which they had incurred by the law-fuit ; and as the greateft proof imaginable of Mrs. Bull's particular favour to them, fhe would admit any of them to vifit her in her own drawing-room, and give them a feat at her card-table. As a token of her fincerity in thefe profeffions, fhe fent feveral prefents to their wives and daughters, and gave the deputies a large purfe of money, to be diftributed-*privately* among the moft influential perfons in the feveral families.

THE deputies had fcarcely alighted, before they fent their footman to the door of the houfe where the heads of the families were affembled, with a meffage of compliments

ments to announce their arrival, and afk permiffion to make a friendly vifit. The porter refufed entrance to the footman, and he returned, without having delivered his meffage. The deputies then wrote the purport of their errand, and fent it to the porter, who delivered it, and the following anfwer was returned—

" GENTLEMEN, we cannot hear any invectives againft our good friend Mr. Lewis. If your mafter is in earneft, tell him that he muft withdraw his action and clear the road. This is all from your humble fervant,
     In behalf of the Forefters,
               H. L. *Chairman.*"

DISAPPOINTED and chagrined, but not wholly difcouraged, the deputies attempted privately to get into fome of the houfes ; but they were refufed entrance. They wrote letters and threw them in at the windows, or put them into the key-holes, but all to no purpofe. The firmnefs and

L   inflexibility

inflexibility of the forefters aftonifhed them, and they were obliged to return with aching hearts, and tell their mafter and miftrefs that the foreft was loft forever.

AND now was verified the old faying,

" Earth has no curfe like love to hatred turn'd ;
" Hell has no fury like a woman fcorn'd."

BUT Madam's fury and its confequences, will be the fubject of my next.

ADIEU.

Letter XIII.

Mrs. BULL's Rage, and its Effect on the Neighbours.—Several Families associate to defend their Right to the High Way.—Quarrel opens with Lord STRUT and Mr. FROG.—The Foresters prosecute their Controversy and obtain a second Verdict.—Mr. BULL's real Friends interpose, and convince his Wife of her Error.—She advises him to compromise the Matter.—He signs a Quit-Claim of the Forest.

DEAR SIR,

NOTHING could exceed the rage into which Mrs. Bull was thrown by this disappointment. "O these cursed, stubborn, ungrateful, disobedient wretches, to refuse all my invitations, and spurn at my offers of friendship, and reconciliation !

L 2   What,

What, not admit my deputies into their houfes ! Did ever any woman fuffer fuch difgrace ? Well, faith, I will be revenged, and
they fhall feel the power of my vengeance.
I will profecute them to the utmoft extremity of the law ; ay, and beyond law too, for
I will fet their houfes on fire over their
heads, and drive them off the land ! And
as to that deceitful dog of a Lewis, I will
raife fuch a hornet's neft about his ears,
that he fhall repent his bargain ! If Lord
Strut attempts to help him, I'll lay an attachment upon his richeft farms. And as
for Nic Frog, if he lends them money, I
will break up his ware-houfe, and fell all
his goods by auction. I will fatiate my
vengeance on the whole pack of them,
and if I fall myfelf among the general
wreck, I fhall have the glory of dying like
Samfon in the ruin of my enemies."

THE rage which Mrs. Bull indulged on
this occafion, and the noife which fhe made
in her raving fits, raifed a great alarm in
the family, and as hyfterics are faid to be
catching,

catching, so the distemper spread into the
two next families, viz. into those of sister
Peg and brother Patrick. The former
imagined that it was Mr. Bull's intention
to call in Lord Peter to his aid, because he
had been of late somewhat complaisant to
those of his natural children, who resided
in the family; and the latter expected that
he should be treated in the same manner
as the foresters, because he had complained
of some restraints and impositions from his
brother John Bull, in respect to his trade
and business, which was that of a linen-
draper. Old jealousies and grudges were
revived on this occasion, and the whole
neighbourhood was in confusion. The
dogs in Peg's family kept a constant howl-
ing and barking, and were answered by
those of Mr. Bull. Several of them actually ran mad,* and Bull was obliged to
place guards at his doors and gates, who
attacked the curs with clubs, and killed several on the spot. In the midst of this hurly
burly, his house was set on fire, and was
                                    actually

* Protestant association, 1779 and 1780.

actually feen blazing in thirty-fix places at once ;* the fire even penetrated Madam's drawing-room, and her card party were obliged to hand buckets and pump the engine; and it was not without the greateft exertions that the whole manfion was faved from utter deftruction.

A DIFFICULTY alfo arofe from another quarter, where it was little expected. The meafure which Mr. Bull had adopted of ftopping the high way, and fearching all carriages, provoked all the neighbours, who thought it a great infringement of their common rights ; but as he was a perfon of fo much wealth and power, they were afraid openly to conteft that point with him. At length an elderly widow lady, of large property, with whom he had always lived on friendly terms, and who generally went by the name of Madam *Kate*, took the liberty to tell him, that fhe could no longer fuffer her neighbours and herfelf to be fo impofed upon ; that the high way

was

* Lord G. Gordon's mob.

was common to all ; that he had no right
to stop passengers and examine them, but
that every body ought to go about their
lawful business without let or hindrance,
and that she was determined to form a
combination* with Mr. Frog, Mr. Lewis,
Lord Strut, and all the other neighbours,
to remove the incumbrances which Mr.
Bull had thrown in the way, and clear the
passage.

THIS combination extended to other objects, besides clearing the high way. They
were all disposed to help the foresters against
Mr. Bull, though in different ways. Lewis
had already lent them money and feed lawyers to plead for them. Lord Strut, though
rich in landed interest, yet generally antici-
pated his revenues, (or as the vulgar phrase
is, ate the calf in the cow's belly) he therefore had no money to spare ; but to oblige
his friend Lewis, he laid an attachment on
a southerly corner of the forest, which for
merly

* Armed neutrality formed by the Empress of
Ruffia, &c.

merly belonged to him; and which from
the numerous flowers with which it a-
bounds, had got the name of *Terra Florida.*
At the fame time he attached one of Mr.
Bull's favourite hunting-feats,* which commanded an extenfive profpect, and was fit-
uate extremely convenient for hunting,
fowling, and fifhing.   It had formerly belonged to Strut, but he had foolifhly loft it
by ftaking it in a game of *whift,* which he
played with Mr. Bull.   It was a doubt in
law whether real eftate could be held by
fuch tenure, but Bull had *poffeffion,* and that
you know is eleven points of the law.   At
any rate, it would oblige Bull to defend ;
and that would coft him money, and divert
fome at leaft of his lawyers from the bufinefs of the foreft.

A SECRET correfpondence had for fome
time been carried on between the forefters
and Mr. Frog, for a loan of cafh, and a
mercantile contract.   Bull had fufpected
it, but could not prove it, till one night,
                                             his-

* Gibraltar.

his myrmidons caught a meffenger from the foreft and fearched his pockets,* in which were found certain letters and other papers, which were fuppofed to amount to full evidence.

UPON this occafion an advertifement was publifhed, according to fafhion, juftifying the meafures about to be taken, and deploring the evils which were connected with them. However fmall a fhare of credit thefe publications obtain, it is generally as much as they deferve.

To make fhort work with Frog, Mr. Bull got a fearch-warrant, and fent a bailiff to his richeft ware-houfe,† who entered it, *per fas aut nefas*, tumbled over the merchandife, under pretence of fearching for ftolen goods; and having taken away as many as he pleafed, by a writ of *venditioni exponas*, he put them up at auction, and it is faid, made a fortune by this job. Mr. Lewis

* Capture of Mr. Laurens.
† St. Euftatius.

Lewis was ·fo exafperated at the outrage thus committed· on his friend Frog, that by a writ of *fcire facius*, he laid claim to the ware-houfe ·and its contents,, and brought in Bull for damages.

In fhort, ·Mr: Bull now found himfelf foufed over head and ears in that deep· ditch, the law.   Like Ifhmael of old, his hand was againft every man, and every· man's hand· againft him.   Look which way foever he would, he found enemies, and his own family were continually buzzing. in his ears, that he would briug his affairs to ruin..

By the affiftance derived from the loans· which they had negociated with Lewis and Frog, and the additional counfellors and: attornies which Lewis employed for them, the forefters purfued the controverfy with· as much vigour as the forms,. delays and uncertainty of the law would permit.   No lefs than four years longer were confumed· in this expenfive ·quarrel, and Mr. Bull's

numerous

numerous retinue of lawyers were employ-
ing themselves in the various chicanery and
tergiverfations of their profeffion, all the
while fattening on the profits of the fuit ;
whilft his debt was growing at fuch a rate,
that he was at his wit's end to keep the
intereft from accumulating as well as the
principal. At length, by a capital manœu-
vre of Pipeweed's grandfon George, aided
by the counfellors of Lewis, the caufe was
brought to a hearing at *York* court, and
the arguments were of fuch efficacy, that a
fecond verdict was given in favour of the
forefters, with large damages. This verdict came fo near to a final decifion, that all
Mr. Bull's friends were convinced he could
no longer maintain an action againft the
forefters ; and fome trufty old fervants
ventured to whifper in Madam's ear that it
was high time to end the controverfy, for
that it could not poffibly be carried any
farther, without bringing the family and
the trade to total ruin.

" LOOK

" Look ye, Madam, (faid they) how all the fchemes which you have laid, have been uniformly defeated ; you have pro-feffed to know the family *fecrets* of thefe forefters ; but thofe fellows who pretended to give you this information have deceived you. In fact, they have no fuch fecrets as your ladyfhip imagines. What has been *openly* told you all along, is the truth, and you ought long ago to have believed it. Now the conviction has forced itfelf upon you, and you can no longer withftand it. The forefters have been defending their title in the law, and they have made it ap-pear fo plainly, that no jury in the world will ever give a verdict againft them. All who are acquainted with new lands, know that the labour attending the improvement of them, is worth ten times more than the land ; and in fact gives the beft title to it. If our mafter will now end the matter by a compromife, he may yet fave fome part of the manor at the northward, where is the beft of hunting and fifhing ; but if he

purfues

pursues the matter any farther, he will lose it all."

THESE faithful remonstrances, enforced by the necessity of the case, began to have some effect on the turbulent mind of Madam. She saw that it was in vain to contend against the opinions of all mankind, and therefore in her next curtain lecture she held a short dialogue with Mr. Bull, thus——

Mrs. B. My dear, I have been thinking whether it would not be best for you to come to a settlement of this long controversy.

Mr. B. (groaning inwardly) So then you have changed your mind, have you?

Mrs. B. Yes, my dear, I find I have been deceived with false information, or I would never have advised you to prosecute the matter so far.

Mr.

Mr. B. Well, but how like a fool fhall I appear to the world, if, after I have threatened and hectored thefe fellows, and fpent fo much money to recover my right, I fhould give it up at this time of day?

Mrs. B. Why you know, my dear, that you have formerly made conceffions to them, becaufe I judged it *expedient.*

Mr. B. Ay, then I retained my claim of *right;* but that will not do now.

Mrs. B. True, my dear, you muft give up your right and title to about two-thirds of the foreft; but you may ftill hold the other third, and I dare fay no-body will conteft your right to that. And as for that part which you give up, you may fay by it as Lewis did of that which you once took from him——"Hang it, it is not worth the keeping; it has always been a bill of coft to me," and the like.

Mr.

Mr. B. I wifh, my dear, you had given me this advice fome years fooner, I fhould have faved my money and my credit too.

Mrs. B. Why, my dear, I tell you I was deceived ; I am as forry as you are for the lofs of the money and of the foreft, but as the cafe is now circumftanced, I think a compromife would be beft.

Mr. B. Well, I will confider of it.

WHEN Mr. Bull had taken the matter into confideration, he thought it beft to wait the iffue of the fuit with Lord Strut about the hunting-feat, for he was loth to lofe that ; and happily for him, when that caufe came to trial, it was argued fo forcibly by his lawyers, that Strut was obliged to give it up. As foon as Bull heard of that, he cried out, " Now is the moment of victory —now is the time for peace." So calling one of his clerks, " Here, fays he, go and fettle the matter with the forefters, or their deputies, on the beft terms that you can."

The

The deputies and the clerk foon came to an agreement, and a quit-claim deed was drawn, defcribing the butts and bounds of the foreft, and diftinguifhing what he gave up to them from what he retained. This quit-claim being properly engroffed, he with a trembling hand and aching heart fubfcribed it, while Madam, ftanding behind him, could not help fhedding a tear at the fight of a tranfaction to which fhe would never have confented but from dire neceffity.

Letter XIV.

The Foresters form a Partnership.—It proves deficient and ineffectual.—Their Clock out of Order.—Their Strong-Box empty.—Disturbances in some of the Families.—A Meeting is called to revise and amend the Partnership.

DEAR SIR,

I WAS loth to break the thread of my narration in my former letters, and you know that we prattling folks love to tell our stories in our own way, which we are under great advantage to do when we are writing letters. But I will now go back to tell you something of the manner in which the foresters managed their domestic affairs during the controversy with Mr. Bull, and for some time after it was closed.

M   WHEN

WHEN they had broken their connexion with him, it was uncertain what connexions they might form abroad, but it was
judged expedient for them to be united a-
mong themselves, that no one family should
connect itself in trade with any merchant or
factor, without the consent of the others.
In short, it became neceffary for them to
enter into a partnership for their mutual
intereft and convenience. To do this was
a nice point, and required much delicacy.
It was to them a new fubject, and they
had an untrodden path before them. After
much confultation and inquiry, their ingenuity fuggefted to them the idea of an
original focial compact. " Why fhould we
(faid they) look abroad for precedents, when
we have enough among ourfelves ? See the
beavers in our own brooks and meadows,
how they work in complete partnerfhip,
each family has its own cell, and a number
of cells are placed in one pond. They
carry on their operations with peace and
unanimity, without even the appearance of
a *mafter*. Here is a perfect republic, a
                                    complete

complete equality, a striking example of order without subordination, of liberty without jealousy, of industry without coercion, of economy without parsimony, of sagacity without overbearing influence Every one knows his own business and does it, their labour goes on with regularity and decency; their united efforts serve the common cause, and the interest of every one is involved in that of the whole. Let us go and do likewise." The hint took, and a plan of CONFEDERATION, as it was called, was drawn up on principles of the purest equality; each family retaining the entire control of its own domestic concerns, without any interference of the others, and agreeing to contribute *voluntarily* its proportion of labour and money to support the common interest.

THIS was, in theory, a very pretty device, exactly suited to a set of people who thought themselves completely virtuous. But as it often happens that great ingenuity exists without much judgment or policy,

so

so it proved here. These foresters did not consider that their intellects were not, like those of the beavers, confined to a few particular objects; that they were not, like the beavers, void of passions and prejudices, void of ambition, jealousy, avarice and self-interest. With all the infirmities of humanity, they were expecting to establish a community on a plan similar to that in which no such deformities can possibly find admittance.

THOUGH for a while, and during the period of the law-suit, when common danger impelled them to keep themselves close together, this plan answered the end better than none; yet *in fact* the notion of *independence* had so intoxicated their minds, that having cast off their dependence on Mr. Bull, they thought themselves independent of all the world beside. When they had got entirely clear of the controversy with him, they were in the condition of a young heir just come of age, who feels proud of his freedom, and thinks he
.has

has a right to act without control.   Each family felt its own importance, and expected a degree of respect from the others, in proportion to its numbers, its property, its exertions, its *antiquity*, and other trifling considerations, which ought never to have had any place in a partnership of complete equality; and in consequence of this intoxicating idea of independence, each family claimed the right of giving or withholding its consent to what was proposed by any or all of the others.

In the club room, among a number of ingenious devices, there was a clock, of a most curious and intricate construction, by which all the common concerns of the partnership were to be regulated.   It had *one* bell, on which *thirteen* distinct hammers struck the hours.   Each hammer was moved by independent wheels and weights, each set of wheels and weights was inclosed in a separate case, the key of which was kept, not as it ought to have been, by the person who represented the family at club, but in

each

each manfion houfe ; and every family
claimed a right either to keep the key at
home or fend it to club, when and by whom
they pleafed. Now as this clock, like all
other automatons, needed frequently to be
wound up, to be oiled and cleaned, a very
nice and particular adjuftment of circumftances was neceffary to preferve the regularity of its motions, and make the hammers perform their functions with propriety. Sometimes one or two of the hammers would be out of order, and when it
came to the turn of one to ftrike it would
be filent ; then there muft be a running or
fending home for the key, and the houfes
being at a confiderable diftance, much time
was fpent in waiting. Sometimes the
meffenger arrived at an unfeafonable hour,
when the family was afleep, or abroad in
the fields, and it would take up a confiderable time to collect them, and lay the cafe
before them, that they might deliberate
and determine whether the key fhould be
fent or not ; and before this could be done,
the clock would get more out of order.

By

By this means, the club was frequently perplexed; they knew neither the hour of the day, nor the day of the month; they could not date their letters, nor adjuſt their books, nor do buſineſs with any regularity.

BESIDES this, there was another inconvenience. For though they had a ſtrong-box, yet it was filled with nothing but bills of parcels, and accounts preſented for payment, contracts of loans, and indentures for ſervices. No money could be had from any of the families, but by their own voluntary conſent; and to gain this conſent there was great difficulty. Some had advanced what they ſuppoſed to be more than their proportion; others had paid leſs. The former would give no more, till the latter had made up their quotas, and there was no authority which could call any one to account, or make him do his duty. Their whole eſtates were mortgaged for the money which they had borrowed of Mr. Lewis and Mr. Frog; and yet they could carry on no buſineſs in partnerſhip.

In

In fact they had formed such an unheard of kind of partnership, that though they could run themselves in debt, yet they could not oblige one another to raise any money to discharge their debts.

EACH family, however, carried on a separate trade, and they contrived to underfell each other, both at home and at market. Each family also had a separate debt, which some were providing means to discharge, and others neglected. In one or two of the families they went to loggerheads among themselves. John Codline's family was, for several days, a scene of confusion and disorder; nothing was seen or heard, but cursing and calling names, kicking shins and pulling nofes. John at first tried to silence them by gentle means, but finding these ineffectual, he at length drew his hanger, and swore he would cut off the ears of the first that should dare to make any more noise. This threatening drove two or three turbulent fellows out of doors, after which the house was tolerably quiet.
Something

Something of the fame kind happened in Robert Lumber's family, but he made fo good a ufe of his fift as quelled the difturbance at once.

In the family of Roger Carrier there feemed to be a predominant lurch for knavery, for he publickly advertifed that he was ready to pay his debts by notes of hand, fubject to a difcount, the amount of which was indefinite, becaufe continually increafing ; and that whoever did not take his pay, when thus offered, might go without. The other families were alarmed at his conduct ; but had no power to oblige him to deal honeftly, and he carried his roguery fo far, as to bid them all defiance.

In this ftate of debility and diftraction, it became neceffary to confult on fome meafures for a better plan of union. They began to be convinced that they were not *beavers*, nor capable of fubfifting in fuch a ftate of fociety as had been adopted from them. Something more energetic was
wanted

wanted to compel the lazy, to check the knavifh, to direct the induftrious, and to keep the honeft from being impofed upon. It had been often in contemplation to amend the mode of partnerfhip; but now the diforders in fome of the families became fo alarming, that though they had been quelled for the prefent, it was uncertain whether they would not break out again, efpecially as one whole family feemed determined openly to patronize roguery. Thefe confiderations ferved to haften the change which had been contemplated. It was accordingly moved in the club, that each family fhould appoint one or more perfons to meet together, and confult upon fome alterations and improvements in the partnerfhip. This meeting was accordingly held, and the refult of it fhall be the fubject of my next letter.

ADIEU.

Letter XV.

A new Plan of Partnership is proposed.—
Arguments pro and con.—It is establish-
ed.—A Chief Steward appointed, with in-
ferior Officers.—Hunting too much in Fash-
ion.—A new Species of Rats introduced.—
Two Families added to the Number of
Partners.

DEAR SIR,

IT is not in my power to give you a
particular detail of the whole proceedings
of the meeting, which was held to reform
the plan of partnership, in the manner of
your parliamentary journalists, who make
speeches for the members, perhaps better
than some of them make for themselves; but
I will endeavour to give you a summary
of

of the principles on which they proceeded.

THE profeſſed deſign of the meeting was to reform and amend the plan; but in fact when they came to examine it, they found themſelves obliged to paſs the ſame ſentence on it that was once delivered concerning the famous poet Alexander Pope, whoſe uſual ejaculation was *God mend me!* "Mend you," ſaid a hackney coachman, (looking with contempt on his dwarfiſh form and hump back) "it would not be half ſo much trouble to make a new one."

A NEW one was accordingly entered upon, and the fundamental principle of it was, not to ſuppoſe men as good as they ought to be, but to take them as they are. "It is true" ſaid they, " that all men are naturally free and equal; it is a very good idea, and ought to be underſtood in every contract and partnerſhip which can be formed; it may ſerve as a check upon ambition and other human paſſions, and put people in mind that they may ſome time or other be called

called to account by their equals. But it is as true that this equality is deftroyed by a thoufand caufes which exift in nature and in fociety. It is true that all beafts, birds, and fifhes are naturally free and equal in fome refpects, but yet we find them unequal in other refpects, and one becomes the prey of another. There is, and always will be, a fuperiority and an inferiority, in fpite of all the fyftems of metaphyfics that ever exifted. How can you prevent one man from being ftronger, or wifer, or richer than another? and will not the ftrong overcome the weak? will not the cunning circumvent the foolifh? and will not the borrower become fervant to the lender? Is not this noble, free and independent crea-ture man, necefiarily fubject to lords of his own fpecies in every ftage of his exift-ence? When a child, is he not under the command of his parents? Send him to fchool, place him out as an apprentice, put him on board a fhip, enrol him in a compa-ny of militia, muft he not be fubject to a mafter? Place him in any kind of fociety whatever,

whatever, and he has wants to be supplied, and passions to be subdued; his active powers need to be directed, and his extravagances to be controlled, and if he will not do it himself, somebody must do it for him. Self government is indeed the most perfect form of government in the world; but if men will not govern themselves, they must have some governors appointed over them, who will keep them in order, and make them do their duty. Now if there is in fact such an inequality existing among us, why should we act as if no such thing existed? We have tried the *beaver* scheme of partnership long enough, and find it will not do. Let us then adopt the practice of another kind of industrious animals which we have among us—Let us imitate the *bees*, who are governed by one supreme head, and, under that direction, conduct their whole economy with perfect order and regularity."

On this principle they drew up an entire new plan, in which there was one chief steward, who was to manage their united interest,

intereſt, and be reſponſible to the whole for his conduct. He was to have a kind of council to adviſe and direct him, and ſeveral inferior oſſicers to aſſiſt him, as there might be occaſion ; and a certain contribution was to be levied on the trade, or on the eſtates of the whole, which was to make a common ſtock for the ſupport of the common intereſt ; and they were to erect a tribunal among themſelves, which ſhould decide and determine all differences. If nine of the families ſhould agree to this plan, it was to take place ; and the others might or might not adopt it ; but if any one ſhould finally refuſe, or if any ſhould adopt it and afterward fall from it, he was to be looked upon as an outcaſt, and no perſon was to have any connexion with him.

THE meeting having continued a long time, every body became extremely anxious to know what they were about ; the doors were kept ſhut, and no perſon whatever was let into the ſecret till the whole was completed.

completed.   A copy was then fent to each family, for them to confider at their leifure.

THOUGH curiofity was now gratified, yet anxiety was not relaxed.   The new plan of partnerfhip went by the name of *the fiddle;* thofe who were in favour of it called themfelves *fiddlers,* and thofe who oppofed it were ftyled *antifiddlers.*   The former faid it was the beft plan that human wifdom had ever contrived.   The latter imagined it " pregnant with mifchief."   The former compared it to a ftrong fence about a rich field of wheat.   The latter compared it to the whale that fwallowed up Jonah.

IN each family a confultation was held on the queftion, Whether it fhould be adopted or not ?   and liberty was given for every one to fpeak his mind with the utmoft freedom.   The objections, anfwers, replies, rejoinders, and rebutters, which were produced on this occafion, would make a curious collection, and form an important

portant page in the hiftory of man. The *fiddlers* were extremely fond of having it examined, becaufe they faid it was like a rich piece of plate, which the more it be rubbed fhines the brighter. The *antifiddlers* faid it was like a worm-eaten bottom of a fhip, the defects of which would more evidently appear, the more it was ripped to pieces; they were therefore for rejecting it at once, without any examination at all.

WHEN they were urged to point out its defects, they would fay, " It is dangerous to put fo much power into the hands of any man, or fet of men, left they fhould abufe it. Our liberty and property will be fafe whilft we keep them ourfelves, but when we have once parted with them, we may never be able to get them back again."

IF the plan was compared to a *houfe*, then the objection would be made againft building it too high, left the wind fhould blow it down. How fhall we guard it againft fire? how fhall we fecure it againft robbers?

N

bers? and how shall we keep out rats and mice?

If it was likened to a *ship*, then it would be asked, how shall we guard it against leaking? how shall we prevent it from running on the rocks and quickfands?

Sometimes it would be compared to a *clock*, then the question was, how shall we secure the pendulum, the wheels and the balance from rust? who shall keep the key, and who shall we trust to wind it up?

Sometimes it was represented by a *purse*, and then it was said to be dangerous to let any one hold the strings. Money is a tempting object, and the best men are liable to be corrupted.

In short, the whole of the arguments against it might be summed up in one word —jealousy; which is well known to be the highest degree of republican virtue.

To

To fhew the futility of thefe arguments, it was obferved by the oppofite party, that it was impoffible to put it into any man's power to do you good, without at the fame time putting it into his power to do you hurt. If you truft a barber to fhave your beard, you put it into his power to cut your throat. If you truft a baker to make your bread, or a cook to drefs your meat, you put it into the power of each to poifon you ; nay, if you venture to lie in the fame bed with your wife, you put it into her power to choak you when you are afleep. Shall we therefore let our beards grow till they are long enough to put into our pock-ets, becaufe we are afraid of the barber ? fhall we ftarve ourfelves becaufe the baker and the cook *may* poifon us ? and fhall we be afraid to go to bed with our wives ? Fie, fie, gentlemen, do not indulge fuch whims : Be careful in the choice of your barbers, your bakers, your cooks, and your wives; pay them well, and treat them well, and make it their *intereft* to treat you well, and you need not fear them.

AFTER

AFTER much debate and difcuffion, fome of the families adopted it without exception, but in others, the oppofition was fo ftrong that it could not be made to pafs, but by the help of certain *amendments*, which were propofed ; and of thefe amendments every family which thought proper to make any, made as many as they pleafed. The new plan with its appendage of amendments, cut fuch a grotefque figure, that a certain wag in one of the families, like Jotham the fon of Gideon, ridiculed it in the following fable.

" A CERTAIN man hired a taylor to make him a pair of *fmall clothes ;* the taylor meafured him and made the garment. When he had brought it home, the man turned and twifted and viewed it on all fides; it is too fmall here, faid he, and wants to be let out ; it is too big here, and wants to be taken in ; I am afraid there will be a hole here, and you muft put on a patch ; this button is not ftrong enough, you muft fet on another. He was going on in this manner.

manner, when his wife overhearing him, said, have you put on the fmall clothes, my dear? No, faid he. How then, replied fhe, can you poffibly tell whether they will fit you or not? If I had made fuch objections to a gown or a pair of ftays before I had put them on, how would you have laughed at my *female* wifdom? The man took his wife's advice, and faved the taylor a deal of trouble."

In like manner, the new plan of partnerfhip was *tried on*, and was found to fit very well. The amendments were thrown by, for future confideration; fome of them have been fince adopted, but they are fo few and fo trifling, as to make no effential difference.

As foon as a fufficient number of the families had adopted the plan, they began to fet it in operation; and unanimoufly chofe for their High Steward and manager, George, the grandfon of Walter Pipeweed. He had ferved them fo faithfully and generoufly

croufly in conducting the law-fuit againft
Mr. Bull, that no perfon was higher in
their confidence.   As he would take no
reward for his former fervices; fo he began
this new bufinefs with a declaration of the
fame kind, and a proteftation that nothing
could have induced him to quit the fweets
of retirement for the toils of public bufinefs, but a difpofition to oblige his numerous friends who had united their fuffrages
in his favour.   Every one who knows him
is fully convinced of the fincerity of his
declarations, and he has perhaps as large a
fhare of the efteem and affection of the
people in thefe families, as any perfon ever
could expect from a courfe of faithful and
friendly offices.

BESIDES him there is an under fteward,
a council of advice, a chief clerk, a cafhier,
and a mafter of the hounds.   The under
fteward is a perfon of a grave deportment,
much reading and ftrict integrity; he has
written a large and valuable treatife on
family government, and was largely con-
cerned

cerned in effecting the compromife with
Mr. Bull. The council of advice are cho-
fen from the feveral families, and confift
of perfons of the beft education, abilities,
and popularity. The chief clerk has the
care of the moft important papers, and the
cafhier keeps the key of the ftrong-box,
which *now* has fomething in it befides paper. By his advice the debts of the company are put into a fair way of being paid,
though fome grumbling ftill fubfifts among
thofe who were obliged to fell their notes
at a difcount. The mafter of the hounds
is an officer, who it was at firft thought
would have very little bufinefs; but as the
wild beafts of the foreft have of late grown
very troublefome, it is fuppofed that he
will have his hands full. There is too much
of a lurch for hunting among many of the
forefters; and fome have not been afhamed
to exprefs their wifhes that the whole race
of wild creatures was exterminated from
the face of the earth. There are others
who ftill continue of the mind, that thefe
animals are a degenerated part of the *human*

fpecies,

fpecies, and might yet be recovered if prop-
per methods were ufed to tame them; but
it is greatly feared, that while the rage for
hunting continues, all fuch benevolent
projects will fail in the execution.

In fome late hunting matches, thefe wild
animals difcovered fo much art and courage, that feveral of the hunters were laid to
fleep in the bed of honour; and the reft
were obliged to take to their heels, that
they might "live to hunt another day."
Some perfons are of the mind that it is not
beft to feek thefe beafts in their dens, but
rather to guard the fields and take care of
the poultry at home.   Others are for pur-
fuing them to the thickeft fhades of the
foreft, and this feems at prefent to be the
prevailing opinion.   What the fuccefs of
it will be, time muft determine.

Since the new partnerfhip has been eftablifhed, hufbandry and trade have been
carried on brifkly; the houfes are full of
good things, and the children are well clad
                                    and

and healthy; but there is one inconvenience which ufually attends a full houfe,
and that is, that *rats* are very numerous,
and a *new fpecies* of them have lately found
their way thither. Some of them are very
fat and fleek, and are not afraid to appear
in open day light; though it is fuppofed
they burrow under ground, and have fub-
terraneous communications from houfe to
houfe. This is an inconvenience againft
which no remedy has yet been found;
though fome people, from their apparent
veracity, are of the' mind that they will ei--
ther prey upon one another, or elfe eat till
they burft.

I HAD almoft forgot to tell you that two
new families have lately been added to the
number of partners. One is that of *Ethan
Greenwood*, a ftout, lufty fellow, born in the
family of Robert Lumber, but married into that of Peter Bullfrog, from whom, after
a long difpute, he has got a good tract of
land, which originally belonged to his own
father, but was furreptitioufly taken pof-
                                        feffion

seffion of by his father-in-law. The other is *Hunter Longknife*; he was bred in the family of Walter Pipeweed, and has a large fhare of his fpirit of adventure. Having taken up his refidence in the outfkirts of the foreft, he has had many a fcuffle with the wild beafts, who are extremely fond of his green corn and young chickens, whenever they can get a tafte of them.

Letter XVI.

Present State of Mr. Bull.—His Wife and his Mother.—Story of the everlasting Taper. —Some Account of Mr. Lewis.—His new Wife and cast off Mistress.—Conclusion.

DEAR SIR,

AFTER giving you such a long detail of the affairs of these foresters, I will close my correspondence, for the present, with a brief account of the situation of the principal persons with whom they are or have been connected, and whom I have had occasion to mention in my other letters.

To begin with Mr. Bull. Though he has given a quit-claim of that part of the forest where his old servants and best customers have possession, yet he retains the northern .

northern part, together with fome hunting-
feats which he *promifed* to give up to the
forefters.   The chief produce of this northern territory is the furs, which are brought
to his ware-houfe and wrought up by his
tradefmen.   Notwithftanding the lofs of
his title to the lands of the forefters, they
have not wholly forfaken him as a trader.
He keeps his fulling-mills at work, and
fupplies them with cloths of various kinds,
but they feel themfelves at liberty either to
purchafe of him or his neighbours, or to
manufacture for themfelves.   He is rather
more complaifant to them in his own fhop,
than his factors are in fome of his diftant
ware-houfes, where they are not allowed to
carry their produce to market, nor to receive coffee, cotton, and fugar, as formerly.
However, they have found out other places
where they can buy thefe commodities
without afking his permiffion.   And as
for that capital article TEA, which was the
occafion of beginning the controverfy, they
now fetch it directly from the original
ware-houfe of old *Cang-hi,* where it is man-
ufactured.

ufactured. They purchafe their filks and muflins of the firft makers and dealers, and get their wines directly from the vineyards.

I HAVE before told you that Mr. Bull formerly ufed to fend the *ordure* made in his family to enrich the plantations of the forefters; but fince his quarrel with them, he has been fomewhat at a lofs how to difpofe of it. At firft he threw it into the gutter* before his door. But there was fuch a large quantity of it, and the ftench which it caufed was fo offenfive, that this expedient would not anfwer the end. He then thought of fending it to a place where fome of his family had been employed in *botanizing*,† in hope that by adding to the fertility of the foil, they would find more encouragement to profecute their inquiries, and that he fhould in time receive fome rent or recompenfe. This fcheme, like fome others, the product of his fruitful brain, has been hitherto attended with more coft
                                                    than

* Convicts employed in lighters on the Thames.
· † Botany Bay, in New Holland.

than profit ; yet it is ftill perfifted in, and great expectations are ftill indulged.

As to his domeftic affairs, his *wife* ftill rules him according to her ufual maxims, and keeps up her gaming club, where fhe wins and lofes alternately ; but between the fhop and the drawing-room, there is enough gained to pay the intereft of his debt, though it is not imagined he will ever be able to pay the principal. This, like a millftone about his neck, muft finally fink him.

You may poffibly be curious to know what is become of his *mother*, whom I have formerly mentioned to you as having had fome fway in his family. The truth is, that fince he married his prefent wife, the old lady found her influence decreafing and retired to her chamber, where fhe has been for many years confined, and is now wholly bed-rid. Mr. and Mrs. Bull, indeed treat the old lady with much decency, and fuffer none to intrude upon her, but fuch

company

company as fhe is fond of. Old Madam
has all the infirmities of age about her.
She will not fuffer herfelf to be touched
nor turned in her bed ; nor the room to be
aired, nor her linen fhifted. She keeps
her window-fhutters clofed, and will not
admit the leaft ray of light in her apart-
ment, but what proceeds from her own
candle, which having been once dipped in
confecrated water, is fuppofed to poffefs
all the virtues of an everlafting taper.

Now I have fpoken of Madam's taper,
perhaps you will be amufed with fome account of it. It is a wax candle of a common fize, fet in an old-fafhioned filver candleftick richly emboffed and gilt; but the
ruft and duft of it are fo facred, that it is
never permitted to be fcoured. The tradition is, that this candleftick formerly belonged to St. Peter, and the candle firft
placed in it, is fuppofed to have been lighted at the sun, and by a myfterious kind of
uninterrupted fucceffion, has been kept burning ever fince. By the light of this taper,

old

old Madam reads her bible and books of devotion, which always lie on a table by her bed-fide.

SOME perfons of an incredulous turn of mind, have pretended to call in queftion this myftery ; but it is ftill held facred by the old lady, and by moft of Mr. Bull's own family. There are fome even among the forefters of the fame opinion ; and fuch is the liberality in thefe families, that no one is molefted in the indulgence of any inno-cent whim, which does not affect the peace of the families, nor the intereft of the part-nerfhip. It was not long after the re-eftab-lifhment of harmony between them and Mr. Bull, that thefe perfons fent two can-dles in one lantern, and one in another, to be lighted at this venerable taper, and dipt in the confecrated water. Two of them were actually lighted in old Madam Bull's prefence, and to her great fatisfaction. The third was lighted at a taper fuppofed to be derived from the fame original, but " hid under a bufhel" in one of fifter Peg's out-houfes,

houfes, it not being permitted to burn publickly in her family, where the only candles
allowed, are of the manufacture of Geneva.

THERE has been as long a controverfy
between different opinionifts on this fubject, as between the fectaries in Liliput,
about breaking the egg at the big or little
end. But it is eafy enough to accommo-
date the matter by granting that St. Peter's
candle, as well as thofe from Geneva, were
originally lighted at the sun ; that the fame
fource of light is open to all ; and that it
is of no confequence of what materials
tapers are made, nor in what kind of can-
dlefticks they are placed, nor by whofe
hands they are lighted, provided they *give
fo clear a light as to anfwer the purpofes of
vifion.*

IT remains only that I give you fome
account of Mr. Lewis. The adventures
in his family have been very fingular. I
formerly told you that he feed lawyers to
plead the caufe of the forefters. Thefe

O   fubtile

fubtile practitioners foon found that the fame arguments which they were obliged to ufe in favour of the forefters, would apply with equal propriety to the cafe of Mr. Lewis's own family. He had long been a widower, and the family was governed by a fucceffion of kept miftreffes, who minded only their pleafures and the enriching of their own relations and dependants. The tenants were abufed, the manfion houfe was dirty and out of repair, and though the rents were paid into the hands of the fteward, yet much oppreffion and embezzlement, and little economy, were the conftant topics of complaint.

AFTER the alteration, produced by the affiftance of Lewis's lawyers in the foreft, they began to think it was high time to do fomething of the fame kind at home. The only peaceable remedy which they could imagine, was to perfuade Mr. Lewis to marry a reputable woman, who would be agreeable to the family. After much argument he was at length brought to fee

the

the neceffity of the cafe ; and, to prevent a
law-fuit, with which they threatened him,
he confented to take the wife which they
recommended. She is a lady of good fenfe
and polite manners, and treats him with
the greateft deference and propriety. She
has had the manfion thoroughly repaired,
the floors and windows cleaned, and the
walls whitewafhed, and is not afraid to let
her inmoft apartments be vifited by the
fun and air. The building is now commo-
dious, wholefome and pleafant, and the
dirty dog-kennel,* which ftood near the
door, is demolifhed.

IT is fufpected by fome that Lewis ftill
has a hankering after his old connexions,
but he profeffes love to his new wife in
the ftrongeft terms imaginable. His caft
off miftrefs has had the audacity to infult
the newly married lady, and tell her that fhe
has no bufinefs to occupy *her* apartments ;
that all Mr. Lewis's profeffions are infincere,
and that *fhe* ftill poffeffes his heart. If
O 2   .   thefe

* Baftile, 1789.

thefe ladies fhould go to pulling caps, Mr.
Lewis will be in a critical fituation, as indeed every man is when two women are
contending for him. It is faid that fome of
the neighbouring gentlemen, who prefer
concubinage to matrimony, have taken the
part of the late miftrefs, and infift on her
reftoration to bed and board; but how this
matter will terminate, can be decided only
by futurity.

HE has alfo been very unfortunate in
fome of his diftant plantations and facto-
ries. His black cattle have caught the horn
diftemper; fome of his farm houfes have
been burnt, and it is thought that feveral
years will intervene before his affairs will
be fet to rights.

THUS, my friend, I have endeavoured to
fulfil my promife by giving you fuch an
account as I have been able to procure of
the forefters and their connexions. I affure
you I am extremely delighted with the
country and its improvements, which exceed

ceed by far the expectations of every perfon who travels this way, and has formed
what he may think a juft idea of the country, by ftaying at home and hearing the reports of others. There is no poffibility of
conceiving what a fine country it is without actually feeing it; I therefore recommend to you a journey hither, for a two-
fold purpofe, viz. to cure you of the fpleen,
and to convince you how much human induftry and ingenuity can perform in a fhort
time, when nature has already done her part
toward making a good country and a happy
people.

Yours, &c.

[The preceding Letters were written 1792.]

Letter XVII.

DEAR SIR,

BEING assured that my former letters have afforded some entertainment to you and your friends, I shall with pleasure resume my pen agreeable to your request, and continue my account of the Foresters and their connexions.

My

My laſt gave you the lateſt information which could then be had, relative to the families of Mr. Bull and Mr. Lewis; and it is proper for me to begin where I left off, becauſe the circumſtances of thoſe two eternal rivals have had ſome influence, and I fear will always have too much on the ſentiments and tranſactions of my favourite foreſters. For, notwithſtanding all that dignity and independence of character which really exiſt among them, and which ought to prevail over every inferior principle, yet there are perſons in all theſe families, who, from local and commercial attachments, or from natural and political connexions, are ſtrongly inclined to imitate the manners and adopt the principles of one or the other of thoſe ancient rivals.

I have told you, that there was a ſuſpicion of a hankering which Lewis indulged toward his caſt off miſtreſs; and that the neighbouring gentlemen favoured the intrigue. This ſuſpicion has been ſadly verified, and a long and bitter controverſy has enſued.

enfued between Lewis and the new wife who had been impofed on him.   Her jealoufy was raifed to a monftrous pitch, and the proofs of his infidelity became fo flagrant, that nothing would fatisfy her but a divorce, not barely *à menfá et thoro* but *à vinculo matrimonii.*   After a long and folemn hearing, the fentence was pronounced in due form, and approved by the major part of the family ; who, in confequence, turned him out of doors.   The minor part, who adhered to him, were fo roughly handled by the majority, that fuch of them as could, were glad to efcape, leaving the reft maimed and wounded on the floors ; which were fo ftained with blood, that they looked as if the famous Doctor Sangrado*, and all his imps had been fully employed in their favourite operation.

SUCH was the noife and uproar on this occafion, that all the neighbours, and efpecially thofe who favoured Lewis's intrigue, were alarmed.   Mr. Bull, whofe choler
you

* See the Adventures of Gil Blas.

you know is very eafily raifed, took this opportunity to fwear the peace againft the whole family of which Lewis was lately at the head. Not content with this, which might have paffed merely for a defenfive meafure, he entered a complaint to the grand jury, and had a bill found againft them "for riotous, routous and diforderly behaviour," and determined to profecute them with the utmoft rigour of the law: For, faid he, within himfelf, " If thefe fellows are fuffered to go on at this rate, they will fet a fine example to their neighbours, and turn every thing upfide down. If the conduct of mafters does not happen to hit the humours of fer-vants, we fhall all be turned out of doors as well as Lewis. Poor devil! I once hated him as heartily as any body; but now he is in diftrefs, I pity him, and can fay as Ahab did to Benhadad, *he is my brother.* If fuch principles and conduct fhould pafs unpunifhed, no mafter can be fure of his property, or power; all family govern-ment is at an end, and a ftrong-box is no fecurity.

fecurity. It is evidently my duty to beftir myfelf; and befides, what a fine opportunity is now prefented to revenge the conduct of this officious family, who meddled in my controverfy with the forefters! Now I will pay them double and round."

To carry this refolve into execution, he entered into articles of agreement with Lord Strut and Nicholas Frog to ftand by him; and gave large fees to the moft able pleaders, particularly to *Ferdinand*, *Frederic* and *Leopold*, who profeffed to have an intereft of their own in fupporting his caufe. Thefe crafty brethren of the long robe, after making a formal parade of their eloquence at the bar, contrived by various pretences and ftratagems, well known in their profeffion, to fpin out the caufe, and require additional fums of money; which Mr. Bull generoufly, and even profufely advanced. For it is a fettled maxim with him, never to fpoil any piece of work for fear of expenfe. This being well known

to

to those whom he employs, they are never
in a hurry to finish a job ; and why should
they, when they have so able and ready a
pay-master.

WHAT became of Mr. Lewis after his
divorce and expulsion, is uncertain. A letter* has appeared, pretending to have been
written by him, which speaks in strong
terms of the ill treatment he has received,
and contains a strange compound of sever-
ity and lenity toward the family. Some
are still of opinion that he may be restored ;
but it is generally thought that he will not
be able very soon to show his *head* again
among his old neighbours.

THE changes which took place in the
family after his expulsion, were numerous
and rapid. The new wife did not long
preserve her dignity, but was frequently
tousled and tumbled by the rude hand of
every frolicksome fellow in the house.
The name of Lewis was expunged from
the

* Manifesto of Louis XVIII.

the fign-board, and in its place was fubfti-
tuted the name of fome remote anceftors
of the family who were called *The Franks*,
and by this firm the houfe is now known.
Various devices were propofed for a new
coat of arms ; one was a wheel within a
wheel, with the word *Jacobina* for a motto.
Another was a bloody *robe* mounted on a
fpear, with the motto, *in terrorem*. But it
feems to be at length determined, that
three plain ftripes of white, red and blue,
fhall be the device, with the motto *une et
indivifible*. Had there been but one colour,
the motto would have been more intelli-
gible.

NOTWITHSTANDING all their inteftine
divifions, and their daily and nightly broils
among themfelves ; yet the Franks have
had the addrefs to fhow a bold face to their
adverfaries, and to defend their caufe in the
law with a refolution truly honourable.
Their refources are fuppofed to be confiderable. Thofe who quitted the family were
not permitted to carry off their clothes and
trunks,

trunks, fome of which contained a valuable booty. The old family plate and jewels, and the ornaments of the devotional clofet, have been fold at auction. The real eftate is in effect mortgaged, by promiffory notes, iffued on its credit, which, though they have greatly depreciated in the market, by reafon of forgeries carried on in Mr. Bull's family, and by his connivance, yet will probably be redeemed at fome rate of difcount at prefent unknown.

The Franks have alfo found means to filence Mr. Bull's moft powerful pleaders, notwithftanding the large fees they received from him. They have even detached Nicholas Frog from his connexions with Bull, and taken him into partnerfhip with themfelves; though it is whifpered that Nicholas is not over and above pleafed with the new mode of *fraternization*, as it hath brought him into a law-fuit with Bull, who at once laid attachments on all his filks and fpices. Lord Strut has alfo difengaged himfelf from the concern; Bull grins hor-
ribly

ribiy at him for his infincerity, and threatens to fieze all his plate and bullion, (of which he has an immenfe quantity) to make good the damage.

HAVING introduced the word *fraternization*, I muft tell you that this is one fpecimen, and there are many others, of that liberty which the Franks have affumed, of coining words. It has been the practice of the family for a long time, and they have been flattered by the frequent adoption and ufe of their new words in other families, who always regarded them as the moft polite and plaufible, if not the moft deeply learned in the whole neighbourhood. When words have a real and definite meaning, it is of no confequence who is the original coiner of them, nor by whom they are brought into ufe; but every one is fond of the productions of his own brain, and every one has a right to claim and enjoy the honour (if there is any) belonging to fuch productions. Never was a word better adapted to any particular purpofe than

than this. To *fraternize*, in the fenfe of the Franks, is to *make brethren ;* to coax, or bribe, or compel, or ufe means of any kind whatever with other people to *make* them brethren.

AFTER the divorce and expulfion of Mr. Lewis, the majority, who affumed to govern the family, were fo intoxicated with the idea of the liberty which they enjoyed in being free from their mafter, in toufling and handling their miftrefs, in picking the locks and fearching the trunks of the deferters, and breaking up the old family hordes, that they began to think this was a kind of liberty which all families had a right to enjoy as well as themfelves. They came therefore to a refolution, to endeavour as far as in them lay, to extend the bleffings of this liberty to their neighbours, beginning with the neareft. They made offers of fervice, either fecretly or openly, to bring on revolutions among them, or as they metaphorically expreffed it, "to plant the tree of liberty in their gardens."

gardens." This was what they meant by *fraternization.* All who favoured their ideas in other men's families were called *democrats,* and thofe who were not fond of the fraternizing plan were termed *ariſto-crats,* words alſo of their own coining. To ſhow their contempt of all titular diſtinctions, they difuſed the appellations of Sir, Monfieur, your Honor, and the like, and ſubſtituted the name of *citizen,* which was ſuppoſed to be equally applicable to all. But to expreſs their own moſt *modeſt* opinion of themſelves, in the loweſt of all poſſible terms, they affected the name of *Sans-culotte,* which in plain Engliſh ſignifies *bare-*****; a word, before this time applied only to thoſe moſt contemptible of the ſpecies who were too lazy to earn enough to buy a pair of ſmall-clothes. To ſuch ridiculous lengths will people go, when they ſuffer their enthuſiaſtic imagination to get the better of their judgment! But the wifeſt have their foibles; and, who is there that cannot recollect, in the courſe of his life, ſome inſtances of indifcretion?

I SHOULD

'I should not have detained your attention fo long to this article, had there not been a very abfurd attempt made to extend the plan of fraternization to the Forefters; who were already the elder brethren of the Franks, both in principle and conduct, and heartily wifhed well to their caufe—But of. this you fhall hear more in my next.

I will only further obferve, at this time, that there has appeared in the family of the Franks, a ftrange kind of zeal on the fubject of *religion*. Before thefe changes took place, Mr. Lewis, and the family in general, entertained a decent, though partial refpect for Lord Peter, and were fond of buying thofe devotional books and trinkets, in which you know he is a large dealer; but fince the expulfion of Lewis, no notice has been taken of the old gentleman, except to infult him, by burning all thofe books and trinkets which they could find in the family, and thus turning his whole trade into ridicule and contempt. To fhew how totally they difregarded all their former

P

received

received opinions, both true and falfe, they have contrived a new almanack, from which all the old red-letter days are expunged, and even the dominical letter is omitted. They have alfo revifed their vocabulary, and erafed the words *revelation*, *refurrection* and fundry others; and by a new infcription on the family tomb, they have declared their difbelief of immortality.* Yet by an unaccountable inconfiftency, they have dug up feveral corpfes, which were very offenfive ;† and exhibited them publickly, in the fame manner as the Romans performed what they called the *apotheofis* of their Emperors. This idle attempt to *annihilate fouls* and to *deify carcaffes*, has not gained them any credit among men of reflection, becaufe neither one nor the other is fuppofed, by fober people, to be within the reach of human power.

It

* " Somme eternel."

† Funeral honours of Voltaire, Rouffeau, and Mirabeau.

IT is faid, and I hope it is true, that the moft confiderate among them are difpofed to throw a veil over thefe tranfactions, and not to make themfelves any more ridiculous, by oppofing opinions which at leaft are innocent, and whch have fome claims to refpect from their antiquity.

ADIEU.

Letter XVIII.

Miſſion of TENEG *from the Franks to the Foreſters.——Deſcription of Mother Carey's Chickens.——Bull's Jealouſy and Choler.—— Prudence of the Foreſters, and its Succeſs. ——Impudent Attempt of the Chickens, and its Defeat.——Bull's Meſſage to Cang-hi, and his ſententious Anſwer.——Peaceable Diſpoſition of the Wild Beaſts.——Agreement with the Iſhmaelites and Lord Strut.——Increaſe of Rats.*

DEAR SIR,

I HAVE already given you ſome idea of the fraternizing ſcheme of the Franks ; I ſhall now inform you of the means by which they attempted to introduce it among the foreſters.

MANY

MANY of the Franks had been in the forest, and had visited the plantations and families there, not only during the law-suit with Bull, but after the dispute had been terminated. They had kept journals and made remarks on manners, economy, husbandry, manufactures, literature, and other things worthy of notice. After they had effected the expulsion of their matter, these travellers were very fond of introducing the same family economy which they had observed among the Foresters, and of extending the blessings of fraternity to them, by drawing them into the controversy in which they were engaged. "Why should not these foresters (said they) bear a part of our burden, as we did of their's. We involved ourselves in their quarrel with Bull, and helped them to terminate it in their favour. One good turn deserves another; and it is now time for them to enter into our controversy, and help us in, the same way."

To

To execute this plan, they difpatched a plaufible, prattling, infinuating petit-maitre, by the name of TENEG, who had been employed in fraternizing the family of CALVINO, a famous diftiller of gin,* and had there been very fuccefsful.

ARTIFICES of the fame kind will not fucceed on all forts of perfons; but a variation muft be obferved, according to the variety of humours, interefts and prejudices. The forefters were well known to be a wary and difcerning, as well as ingenious kind of people, and fond of novelties. To hit their ruling paffion, and thereby influence or deceive their judgment, Teneg was furnifhed with a bafket of birds' eggs, of a new fpecies, which had recently appeared in the gardens of the Franks. Of thefe birds, I cannot give you the name and defcription, nor do I know whether they are included in any of the claffes found by naturalifts; but to fpeak in the vulgar phrafe they are known, in fome places, by the

* Gin is an abbreviation of Geneva.

the name of *war-hawks*; rather improperly, I think, becaufe the hawk though a ferocious is yet a filent bird ; whereas thefe are fo very noify that they feem to belong to the pettrel tribe, and have been not improperly called *Mather Carey's Chickens*, from their refemblance to a bird of that name, which is well known to chirp and whiftle at the approach and during the height of a ftorm.

THESE birds have fome peculiarities, which muft be confidered as characteriftic of the fpecies. One is, that they vary their note according to the inftruction of their keepers ; in this refpect they refemble the magpye and the mock-bird. Their ufual found, when not under any particular direction, is a dull monotony, an eternal repetition of *jaco, jaco, jaco*; but they have been taught to found other words which terminate with a vowel, or a liquid confonant ; fuch as, *war, war, war* ;—*whifky, whifky, whifky,* —*ja, ja, ja,* &c. If they chance to hear the whetting of a knife, or the fnapping of a trigger,

trigger, or any noise which feems to be a preparation for mifchief, they will readily imitate it, and the found will catch from one to another like a feu-de-joye. It is furprifing to fee how eafily they can be trained and difciplined. Teneg, with a bird-call, which he carried in his mouth, could bring them by dozens to light on his head and fhoulders, and even dive into his pocket, to pick the grains which he carried there to feed them. He could make them flutter about him in all directions, and imitate any noife which he was pleafed to make. It is faid, that he has imparted this fecret to fome choice fpirits, his affociates.

ANOTHER peculiarity of thefe birds is, that they feem to have an averfion to fome particular days, and a predilection for others. On the twenty-fecond of February they are fcarcely ever feen on the wing, and are remarkably filent; but on the tenth of Auguft, and the twenty-fecond of September, they appear in great numbers, and are heard to whiftle through the

whole

whole day. The caufe of this peculiarity
is one of the fecrets of nature, which, it is
hoped, the learned will in time be able to
penetrate. The vulgar fuppofition is, that
their hilarity in the months of Auguft and
September is owing to the great quantity
of the feeds of water-melons, which are
then to be found, and of which they are
faid to be remarkably fond. But this is
altogether a vague conjecture, and unwor-
thy of a philofophic mind.

You will now be ready to afk, how were
thefe eggs to be hatched? and what ufe
could be made of the birds if they fhould
be hatched? To the firft, I anfwer—Tencg
was well informed that there were certain
old hens in the foreft, who would readily
perform the office of incubation. To the
fecond—By a due-management of the birds,
and principally by the force of their notes,
it was expected that they would excite in
the forefters, and their children, the fame
difpofition to mifchief, with which themfelves

felves were poffeffed, and thus prepare the way for a complete *fraternization*.

TENEG arrived firft in the plantation of Charles Indigo ; where he placed fome of his eggs under an old hen, and fcattered the feeds of a particular fpecies of grain, on which the chickens were to fubfift till they could pick for themfelves.   So prolif- ic was the brooding warmth of the old hen, that the eggs were foon hatched, and the chicks began their natural cry, *jaco, jaco, jaco ;* but were foon taught the note *war, war, war.*   The effect was fo furprizing, that feveral of Mr. Indigo's domeftics im- mediately roared out the war-whoop, equip- ped themfelves in the habit of highway- men, and took to the road, with a view to rob any of Mr. Bull's family, or plunder any of his waggons, which they might chance to meet in an unguarded and de- fencelefs ftate.

TENEG was fo flufhed with this fuccefs, that he hafted to the other plantations, dif-
tributing

tributing the eggs with his own hands, or
fending them by trufty meffengers, who
were well acquainted with the nefts of the
old hens. A brood was foon hatched in
each of the plantations, who began their
cackling as foon as they were out of the
fhell. The effect was not fo great in all
parts, as it was in Indigo's plantation; for
though the mufic excited feveral perfons to
kick up a war-dance, and become knights
of the highway ; yet the number was far
greater who faw through the artifice, and
combined to defeat it. Still, however, the
noife of the chickens was continued, and
the highwaymen became fo impudent, that
when Mr. Bull heard what was doing, he
began to fwell with choler againft the for–
efters. " Curfe thefe fellows, (faid he) do
they intend to aid the Franks againft me ?
I'll begin with them betimes. The highway is mine ; I'll feize their waggons,
and ruin their *carrying trade* ; and if
they have a mind for another law-fuit, I
am their match." Accordingly, as lord
of the manor, he fent out his huntfmen
and

and hounds, feized feveral of their waggons and drove them into inclofures, where
they might be fecured till a court-manor
could be holden for *adjudication* upon them.

THE moft confiderate among the forefters were greatly incenfed, on account of the
plots thus formed againft them. Though
they refpected the family of the Franks,
and rejoiced at their emancipation from
the old abfurd fyftem of family government, under which they had long groaned ;
though they made no fcruple publickly to
own them as friends and brethren ; yet
they could not approve all the whims and
innovations, which had crept into the family ; nor did they relifh the plan of fraternization, as the Franks intended to carry it
on. They hated the cackling of the chickens, and wifhed they had perifhed in the
fhell : but they were loth to quarrel with
the whole family for the folly and vanity
of their fervant; efpecially as thofe who
had the principal hand in fending him were
in difgrace, and another fet had got the di-
re&ion

rection of the houfe.   They had at the
fame time a high refentment againft Bull
for feizing their waggons, but thought the
beft way of getting them back again was
by remonftrance and perfuafion.   In thefe
circumftances, a confultation was held by
the council of advice, at which prefided
their trufty High Steward, GEORGE, the
grandfon of Walter Pipeweed, than whom
there is not, perhaps, a man who carries
more wifdom in his head, more goodnefs
in his heart, or more vigour in his nerves.
George has had enough of law-fuits ; and
though he will fuffer no man to wrong him
with impunity, yet he had rather compromife difficulties than inflame them by oppofition.   The refult of the confultation
was, that a letter be written to the Franks,
in a very friendly ftyle, complaining of
Teneg, and requefting that a better man
might be fent in his place ; that a fpecial
meffenger be fent to Bull, to demand fatif-
faction for the damage they had fuftained
from his huntfmen ; at the fame time dif-
claiming the conduct of the highwaymen ;

and

and declaring that they did not intend to meddle with the quarrel between Mr. Bull and the Franks ; but to be in friendſhip with both,. and trade with both as uſual.

No ſooner was this determination known, than thoſe who had the direction of the chickens, ſet them on raiſing a terrible cry, of *war, war, war—ja, ja, ja.* This was very troubleſome and provoking ; but it was thought moſt prudent to bear with their impertinent vociferation for a while, in hope that they would ſoon quit the plantations. For as they had come in all at once, it was not known but that they were birds of paſſage, and might diſappear at the ſeaſon of migration ; but even if they ſhould continue, there was an expectation that means might be found to tame and ſilence them, and perhaps render them in ſome degree uſeful.

An experiment of this kind was actually made. A flock of theſe chickens, under the direction of a miſchievous old hen,

once

once got into a field of William Broadbrim, on the weftern fide of his plantation, and fet up a cry of *whifky, whifky, whifky.* The noife was fo very loud, and their number was fo large, that it was feared they would devour the crop, then almoft ripe for the fickle. A company of archers was therefore fent out, with orders to try the effect of fome particular founds, before they fhould difcharge their arrows. They crept along, making feveral kinds of noife, to no purpofe, till they had got very near, when they fet up a loud cry of *Wafh, Wafh, Wafh;* which entirely drowned the noife of *whifky,* and was fo formidable to the chickens, that they flew away with precipitation, and became remarkably filent. They have not only made no more difturbance in that quarter, but fome of them have fince been obferved hovering about the barn-yards, and mixing with the common poultry.

THE letter fent to the Franks was well received, and produced the defired effect. Teneg was difqualified and fuperfeded ; but

but he did not think it proper to return, left he fhould lofe his ears. He has fince married a girl of the family of Peter Bullfrog, and taken up his abode in the foreft; and, fuch is the good-natured policy of thefe people, that he is permitted to refide among them, and to enjoy what he has earned, without any inquiry how he came by it; provided that he pays his taxes and lives peaceably.

THE meffenger who went to Mr. Bull, was a long time in confultation with his clerk, before all matters could be adjufted to mutual fatisfaction. The refult, however, was a tolerable compromife; in which Bull engaged to give up the hunting-feats which he had fo long withheld, on condition that the *whole* body of the forefters fhould become bound to pay the balance of an old account, due to him from the *fouthern* planters. He alfo promifed to let the difputed limits be adjufted by a committee; to expedite the manor-courts, in which the trefpaffes fhould be fairly tried; and to

pay

pay damages if awarded.   Other matters
which had been in difpute were adjufted ;
but one claufe was inferted, which prohib-
ited them from trading at his fugar ware-
houfe, unlefs they fhould carry their produce in waggons of no larger fize than a
wheelbarrow.   This article was fo fingular
and ridiculous, that the council of forefters
rejected it.   The other parts of the agreement met the approbation of twenty out of
thirty, which made the inftrument valid,
and it was figned, fealed, publifhed and
declared in due form.

As foon as this tranfaction was known,
and even before the inftrument was execu-
ted, thofe choice fpirits whom Teneg had
inftructed, as aforefaid, in the ufe of the
bird-call, fet all the chickens a crying *jo,
ja, ja—treaty, treaty, treaty.*   The found
rang through the foreft, and was reverber-
ated from houfe to houfe, and from tree to
tree, in fuch a furprizing manner, that no
other noife could, for a while, be heard.
Some very fober people were actually deaf-
ened;

Q

encd; others were vexed with the clamour. But confidering from what caufe it proceeded, they determined to let the chickens cry till they were weary; and then calmly and coolly to examine the reafons which influenced their keepers thus to fet them a cackling. This examination has been done in a very mafterly manner; and the people in general are pretty well fatisfied with the compromife. They fee, that though it is not altogether to their wifhes, yet it is the beft bargain that could be made. They fee that it has prevented a long law-fuit, the iffue of which muft have been uncertain; and they had rather enjoy the bleffings of cultivation and of fending their produce to market, than fpend their money in paying council, attornies, folicitors, fcriveners and bailiffs; of which kind of drudgery they have already done enough to make the prefent generation fick of fuch bufinefs.

THERE remained one effort more, which the difciples of Teneg were determined to make,

make, to prevent the agreement from being carried into effect. It was neceffary that a fum of money fhould be allowed for traveling charges, clerks' fees, and other incidental expenfes. When this matter came to be debated in the council of advice, a flock of the chickens, who had been trained for the purpofe, flew into the hall, perched on the table and chairs, and began to cackle with a new note in addition to their former vociferations. *Papers, papers, papers.* Two of them had the impudence to alight on the fhoulders of the High Steward, as he fat mufing in his elbow-chair, and, putting their bills into his ears to fquall this harfh note. GEORGE bore it a while calmly, and continued his contemplations ; till, at length, with his deep grum voice, and with a determined air and manner, he pronounced the monofyllable *No*, fo forcibly, that the cackling ceafed, and the chickens retired to their managers, for farther inftruction. Their invention was ready, and fome pains were taken to teach them the fame monofyllable *No*, with the addition of the word

word *fupply*. This was the moft difficult tafk which had yet been attempted; and it took them fo long to learn it, that the neighbours, who obferved what was going on, had time to *blow the horn*, to call the people together, and put an end to the in- fults of this noify brood.. At the found of the horn, the chickens were frightened; fome to fave their necks from being wrung, flew off in various directions;. others hid themfelves and remained filent; till the council had finifhed their deliberation, and: voted the money. The only ill confequence of this difturbance, was a little delay in the execution of the agreement, which all good: men had the candour to impute to the true caufe.

Notwithstanding all the appearance of good will on the part of Mr. Bull, there are many who think he ftill looks with an envious eye on the Forefters, and is jealous of their enterprizing fpirit, and of their extenfive and growing commerce.. Their agents and factors are feen in all
                                                                    thofe

thofe ware-houfes, from which he had been
ufed to fetch commodities by wholefale,
and difpofe of them by retail at very advanced prices. There is no place to which
they cannot find as ready accefs as himfelf,
and where they cannot trade on equal
terms. It is not long fince he fent a very
pompous meffenger to old Cang-hi, the tea
manufacturer, with his compliments, requefting that he might have fome *exclufive*
advantages in trade, at his ware-houfe ; and
to ingratiate himfelf the better, this meffenger carried a number of valuable prefents,
which, it was thought would be highly ac-
ceptable. The old gentleman received the
meffenger, and fome of the prefents, with
his ufual politenefs ; but obferving the
fupercilious air of the meffenger, he quick-
ly difmiffed him with this fententious reply. " My anceftors have taught wifdom
to their defcendants. Their pictures and
their maxims are delineated in this book,
which I prefent to thy mafter. Tell him
there is no friendfhip in trade. My doors are
open to all cuftomers, and every man is welcome for his money." WHEN

WHEN the Foresters heard of this sagacious reply, they could not help laughing in their sleeves, at the mortification which old Bull must have received from it.

You will wish to know on what terms these people are with the wild beasts on their western border. Since I wrote to you concerning them, a strong hunting party has been sent out, who have driven them from their old haunts, and have erected lodges in the most convenient places, where future huntsmen may reside. But as the creatures appear to be less formidable, and their ferocity is evidently in the *wane*, it has been thought best to entice them to peace, and admit them to familiarity. The old practice is revived of setting molasses for them to lick, and furnishing them with collars and nose-jewels. But above all, a line has been drawn, beyond which no person is permitted to make any plantation. This precaution is one of the best which could be invented, and it is hoped will have so good an effect, as to keep the neighbours out of fear of being devoured.

BESIDES

BESIDES the compromife with Bull, the Forefters have concluded an agreement with two of the Arabian rovers, Muley* and Haffan,† which ftipulates that they may go about their bufinefs without molef-tation, on the payment of a certain fum down, and an annual acknowledgment be-fides. This is a cheaper way of dealing with fuch old rogues, than to let them rob and plunder at their own pleafure. For they are the genuine children of Ifhmael, whofe " hand was againft every man, and every man's hand againft him."

AN advantageous agreement has alfo been made between the Forefters and Lord Strut, adjufting the limits of his foreft and theirs, and opening a road between them, which is to be free to both parties. Mr. Bull has quietly and honourably given up the hunting-feats, according to the agree-ment, and the Forefters are in peaceable poffeffion of them. This will enable them to extend their plantations and cultivate
their

* Morocco.   † Algiers.

their country to the greateſt advantage. They are continually making improvements by bridges and canals ; and if they ſhould continue at peace among themſelves, uninfluenced by the quarrels, and untainted by the diſſipation and folly of their neighbours, they will be as happy a ſet of people as any on the globe. ~ADIEU.

P O S T S C R I P T.

IN one of my former Letters I told you of a new ſpecies of *rats*, which had appeared in the foreſt. I am ſorry to ſay that they not only remain, but are very numerous and miſchievous. They are ſo ſly and evaſive, that they elude all the arts of common rat-catchers ; and at the ſame time are ſo bold and impudent as to make their appearance in open day-light, in the houſes, roads and fields. Not long ſince, a large number of them were ſeen in the dining-room of *George Truſty* ; firſt ſitting under the table, and catching every crumb which fell ; then leaping on the table, whilſt the family were at dinner, and ſnatching the meat out of their plates. George profeſſed great indignation at this degree of impudence, and ſwore that he would permit no ſuch thing in his houſe ; but ſome people are ſo uncharitable as to ſuppoſe this to be only a fineſſe, and that he ſecretly favours them, for ſome occult purpoſes. Should this imagination prove to be well founded, it is thought that his name will be changed ; and that inſtead of being called *Truſty*, he will have a name as long as thoſe uſed in Oliver Cromwell's time, *Better known than truſted.*

www.ingramcontent.com/pod-product-compliance
Lightning Source LLC
Chambersburg PA
CBHW020109030726
47498CB00006B/2022